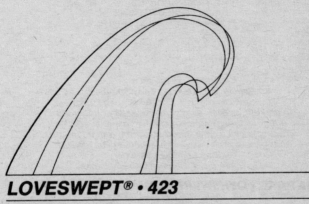

LOVESWEPT® • 423

Erica Spindler
Rhyme or Reason

BANTAM BOOKS
NEW YORK • TORONTO • LONDON • SYDNEY • AUCKLAND

RHYME OR REASON

A Bantam Book / September 1990

LOVESWEPT® and the wave device are registered trademarks of Bantam Books, a division of Bantam Doubleday Dell Publishing Group, Inc. Registered in U.S. Patent and Trademark Office and elsewhere.

If you would be interested in receiving protective vinyl covers for your Loveswept books, please write to this address for information:

Loveswept
Bantam Books
P. O. Box 985
Hicksville, NY 11802

ISBN 0-553-44054-3

Published simultaneously in the United States and Canada

"Fried chicken, Alex? I thought you were a health nut," Walker said.

Alex narrowed her eyes a little. "I am. Fried chicken is one of my weaknesses."

Walker laughed; the sound was low and impossibly suggestive. "Interesting." He drew the word out as he leaned forward. "You must have other . . . weaknesses. What could they be?" He trailed a finger across the back of her hand. "I'd guess moonlight through lace curtains"—he reached the juncture of her thumb and first finger and dipped his finger inside to tease the sensitive flesh—"or maybe the first pungent flowers of spring." He traced the shape of one nail, then another. "Of course there's always bluesy music on hot, still nights or slow, deep kisses that steal not only your breath"—he paused—"but your sanity as well."

Her mouth was dry, her pulse fast. Her hand trembled under his. As hard as she tried not to, all she could think about were his lips, untamed and insistent on hers, and his hands, hot, demanding, and—

"How about it, Alex?" He laced his fingers through hers. "Let's spend the afternoon discovering weaknesses we didn't even know we had. . . ."

WHAT ARE *LOVESWEPT* ROMANCES?

They are stories of true romance and touching emotion. We believe those two very important ingredients are constants in our highly sensual and very believable stories in the *LOVESWEPT* line. Our goal is to give you, the reader, stories of consistently high quality that may sometimes make you laugh, sometimes make you cry, but are always fresh and creative and contain many delightful surprises within their pages.

Most romance fans read an enormous number of books. Those they truly love, they keep. Others may be traded with friends and soon forgotten. We hope that each *LOVESWEPT* romance will be a treasure—a "keeper." We will always try to publish

LOVE STORIES YOU'LL NEVER FORGET
BY AUTHORS YOU'LL ALWAYS REMEMBER

The Editors

I dedicate this book to my miracles:
Nicholas, my son
Nathan Hoffman, my husband
Rita Spindler, my mother

And to love,
the greatest miracle of all

One

Today was the day. Alexis Stanton Clare—Alex to everyone but the equally stuffy Stantons and Clares—lifted her chin, narrowed her eyes, and strode determinedly past the resort's Olympic-size swimming pool. 'Sam' might be one tough hombre, but *today* she would beat him at his own game . . . or die trying.

The late afternoon Arkansas sun was weak but still warm enough to draw the most devoted sun worshipers to the chaise lounges circling the pool. Women all, they lounged in hundred-dollar bits of fabric and string and cast curious glances as Alex moved past.

She brushed at her dusty khaki shorts. She didn't mind their stares, she knew she was as out of place at this high-priced resort as they would be in her tiny cabin in the woods. Her white T-shirt, hands, and legs were stained an orange-pink from her morning's work and her hiking boots were caked with the same orangy soil.

She shook her head, one corner of her mouth

lifting in wry amusement. She could almost hear her mother's voice, cultured in the way of only women from the best southern families—"Alexis Stanton Clare, ladies most certainly do *not* play in the dirt." Nor would they wear hiking boots, men's undershirts, or quartz crystal charms, Alex thought. She considered herself pretty lucky to be doing all of the above—and getting paid for it.

When she reached her destination, she stopped and took a deep breath. Today was the day, she told herself again, smiling in anticipation. She *could* do it. Letting out her breath in a rush, she pushed through the saloon-style doors and faced her opponent—a ten-year-old pinball machine named *Gunslinger Sam*.

The room was dim and, without air conditioning warm; and it smelled faintly of chlorine and must. At the moment, *Sam* had another challenger, a young girl. From her expression, Alex knew she wasn't faring well against the nefarious outlaw.

Alex sauntered over to the machine and put a quarter on its glass top. The girl lifted her eyes for a second and her ball slipped past her paddles.

"Darn."

"Tough luck," Alex said sympathetically. "Do you have another quarter?"

Pink slid up the girl's cheeks. "Yes."

"Go for it."

She did and for several minutes Alex watched her. The youngster looked to be about nine or ten. She was pretty, with soft features. Her long chestnut-colored hair was pulled away neatly from her face with a shiny pink ribbon, not a strand was out of place. Alex thought of her own unrestrainable mane of red hair and grinned.

This girl was the type of daughter her own mother had always wanted.

She lost another quarter, sighed, and stepped away from the machine. "I give up."

"I know how you feel, he's one crafty dude."

"Pardon?" The girl's expression was both shy and curious.

"Sam." Alex motioned toward the picture on the machine, of a cowboy so gritty and tough, he looked as if he ate nails for breakfast and spit them back out after lunch. "He and I have gone head to head on many occasions."

"You've never won?"

"Nope. But I will." Alex sidled up to the machine. "And today's the day."

"Really?" The girl moved a step closer. "How do you know?"

Alex flashed her a smile. "With a guy like Sam, you have to be cocky." She slipped her quarter into the slot, then pulled back on the spring lever. Within a second the ball was up the channel and rocketing off the bumpers. Alex threw herself into the game, rocking and jiggling the machine as she manuvered the paddles.

Several minutes later the ball slipped by her, and she frowned. She would have to do better than that to beat him.

She glanced back at the youngster. "You know, I was watching your technique and I think I could give you a few pointers. Interested?" When the girl nodded, Alex pulled back on the lever and let the ball fly. "You have to put your whole body into it and get aggressive. But know how far to push, because if you go beyond that you'll tilt and lose it all. See . . ." Alex shifted so she was leaning slightly forward, then using the weight of her body she shook and rocked the machine, careful not to cause it to tilt. "Use your hips if you have to"—she demonstrated a sideways thump with hers—"but *never* take your eyes off the ball."

Lights blinked, bells rang, the ball remained in play. The action was lightning fast, and Alex knew that this time she really *did* have him. Her second ball dropped, she fired out her third.

Minutes passed, points mounted. Alex laughed out loud as the machine started clicking over free games.

"You did it!" the girl exclaimed when it was over. "You won four games! Just like you said you would!"

Alex laughed again and lifted the hair off her damp neck. "Yeah, but I've been saying that for weeks. I think you're good luck. Come on, I'll buy you an ice cream to celebrate."

The girl's smile faded. "Aren't you going to stay and use your free games?"

"Naw. I couldn't top this one. Besides, it's hot in here." She held out her hand. "Come on, I'll treat."

The youngster held back. "I'm not supposed to have much sugar."

Yuppie parents, Alex thought, lowering her eyes to the girl's designer shorts outfit. It was as immaculate as the rest of her; her white sandals looked as if they'd never seen a garden path, let alone a mud puddle. "Okay then, forget the ice cream. Let's walk down to the lake and dip our toes in the water."

"I shouldn't." The girl's shoulders slumped. "I'm not allowed by the lake without my father. Besides, I promised him I wouldn't leave the arcade."

She looked positively dejected and Alex battled back a flash of anger. She knew all about overprotective, controlling parents. Too well.

"I'll just stay here . . ." The girl's voice trailed off and the word she didn't say hovered in the air between them. *Alone*. In that moment Alex knew this child spent entirely too much time alone. And that she needed a friend.

It was none of her business, Alex told herself. This girl had parents; it would be wrong of her to try and interfere with their wishes. She should give the girl the free games and walk away. Alex sighed. She'd never been any good at taking advice, even when it was her own.

"Come on, we'll go sit by the pool and pretend it's the lake." She grinned and held out her hand once again. "And while we're at it, we can pretend there's no sugar in ice cream. What do you think?"

Lacy—that was the girl's name, Alex learned later—had thought that was a fine idea and they'd lapped at their chocolate cones as they dangled their feet in the cool, chlorinated water.

Lacy had told her she was from Boston and lived with her father, who was a doctor, and that they were here for an extended vacation. She didn't mention her mother, and Alex didn't ask. They spent about thirty minutes together, the conversation had been light and friendly—an adult and a child getting to know one another.

Then, when Alex had shaken Lacy's hand goodbye, *it* had happened.

It. Her gift, her curse . . . her ability to feel another's pain.

Alex frowned. Lacy's touch had stunned her. Sometimes it happened that way—an immediate reaction to a person, a physical call for help so strong it was like a shout. She wasn't sure she'd felt it so keenly before. Something was terribly wrong with Lacy, something more than being lonely or overprotected.

She had to help her.

Alex looked down at her hands. They trembled slightly, and she silently swore. Two years ago she'd vowed to ignore this "gift" of hers and let people heal themselves. She'd managed to keep her vow by avoiding any type of attachments or involvements, by hiding herself away in the woods. And she'd been happy. She'd been safe.

Disappointed in herself, Alex curled her fingers into her palms. She was a coward. She'd jerked her hand away from Lacy's as if the child had been contagious.

She'd been afraid.

Angry at her own reaction and determined to overcome it, Alex focused on the image of Lacy's sweet, hesitant smile and vulnerable brown eyes. A moment later the phantom pains returned—a burning in her throat, a gnawing ache in her chest. They took her breath away, and she lay back against the grass, the flat of her hand pressed against her stomach.

After several moments, the sensation passed. Alex plucked a blade of grass and rubbed it between her fingers. It felt velvety against her skin, and she held it to her nose to catch the subtle scent that reminded her of every one of her childhood summers.

Thoughts of her childhood brought their own discomfort, and Alex dropped the piece of grass and laced her fingers together. This gift of hers allowed her to feel another's pain, assimilate their confusion, their despair. And when that happened, how could she not become totally involved?

She couldn't. It was as simple as that.

But this time, somehow, she wouldn't be hurt.

Two

Walker Chadwick Ridgeman checked his watch for the fourth time that morning. It was eight-thirty, still too early to pay a call on that Alex woman's crystal shop.

He dragged his fingers through his dark, wavy hair, tamping back his impatience, his annoyance. He hadn't liked hearing that a strange woman had befriended his daughter, he liked it even less that she had encouraged Lacy to break several of his rules. And now he hated waiting for the confrontation.

When she'd returned home the night before, Lacy had held up a quartz crystal with excitement. It was a small thing, not worth more than a dollar. But it wasn't the worth of the item that mattered, it was the principle—Lacy wasn't to accept gifts from strangers, not ever.

He glanced over to the couch where his daughter slept. At the same moment love washed over him, so did frustration and a feeling of helplessness. Walker balled his hands into fists. Why Lacy? Hasn't his sweet, beautiful daughter endured enough pain in her ten years?

He drew in a deep, calming breath, then released it. Crossing to his daughter, he tenderly touched her cheek. He had to let go of his anger and learn to live with the truth—Lacy was a narcoleptic and would, most probably, never recover.

Not without a miracle anyway. Walker shook his head, still stroking his daughter's cheek. Narcolepsy wasn't a life-threatening disease, but it wasn't curable either. And as much as he might wish for one, he was a doctor; he knew incurable conditions remained that way and miracles were found only in the Bible.

There was a knock at his door. Walker drew his eyebrows together, both at the fact that anyone would be calling on them so early and at the sound that accompanied the knock, a strange scruffling as if a dog were scratching at fleas.

It *was* a dog, Walker realized in surprise as he opened the door. The biggest, hairiest, silliest looking one he'd ever seen.

The same couldn't be said for the woman beside him. She was stunning. Her hair was the color of fire and fell away from her face in wild waves, stopping just past her shoulders. Her eyes were those of a dreamer, large and the clear green of a summer lawn. They so dominated her face that at first glance he hadn't noticed her strong cheekbones or generous mouth. Her skin was smooth and pale; freckles abounded across her rather perky nose.

Hers weren't traditional good looks. He supposed she couldn't even be called beautiful. But there was something vibrant about her, something natural and wholesome—a sort of earthy sensuality.

The flame-haired woman smiled. "I hope you have coffee."

"Excuse me?"

"To go with the blueberry-bran muffins." She held up a basket covered with a plaid napkin. "I made them myself."

Walker arched his eyebrows as only a fifth-generation Bostonian could. He didn't know who this woman was or what she and her beast wanted, but he'd been up with Lacy three times the night before and enough was enough. "That's very nice, but—"

"Alex!"

Lacy's squeal was ear piercing. Stunned, Walker studied the woman more closely. *This* was the woman? What had happened to the gray-haired busybody in orthopedic shoes he'd been imagining?

"Hi, Lacy." The woman ducked by him and, he was left gazing at the empty doorway. "Heinz and I decided to stop by."

"This is your dog?" Lacy asked. "He's neat!" Walker turned around in time to see Lacy drop to her knees and throw her arms around the hairy beast. The dog immediately covered her face with appreciative kisses. Walker was too stunned to speak. When had Lacy become so fond of dogs?

"Dad! Can I go out and play with him?"

"I don't know—"

"He's very gentle with children," Alex called as she made a beeline for his kitchen. "Just a big baby himself." She began rummaging through the cabinets. "Walker, do you have any herb tea?"

"No, I—"

"Dad, please!"

"Any decaffeinated coffee?"

Walker sighed and dragged his hands through his hair. All three of them—counting the dog—were staring at him expectantly. "Yes, Lacy, you may go out and play as long as you stay right by the cottage. No, I don't have any herb tea or any decaf."

Alex clucked her tongue. "You're a doctor, you should know how bad caffeine is for the body. Here, Lacy, take a muffin with you—" she tossed her one—"but watch out for Heinz, he loves—"Too late. The dog jumped, caught the muffin in mid-air, and started to run. Lacy squealed again and took off after him. "To play catch," Alex finished calmly, then turned and began filling the kettle with water.

The dog barked and whizzed by him with Lacy in hot pursuit; the woman hummed as she poked around in his refrigerator. Walker took it all in, unsure whether he should be outraged or amused.

With a shake of his head, he stalked to the patio doors and yanked one open. "Lacy, you and that beast outside!" A second later, Lacy raced by him, followed by the dog. That done, he turned and glared at the woman. "Now, can you tell me what the hell's going on?"

"I'm making coffee . . . well, actually, I'm heating water. All you had was instant."

There was an accusatory note in her voice about the limited beverage selection. He fought off his amusement. "I know that. Why are you here making coffee in the first place?"

"To go with the muffins," she said simply, starting toward him with the basket.

Walker ran a hand across his forehead. He'd left himself open for that one. "Let me rephrase the question, why are you here at all?"

Alex swallowed a laugh as she set the muffins on the coffee table. She'd planned to throw him off-balance then stick her nose where it didn't belong before he realized what she was up to. So far, her strategy seemed to be working. The poor guy didn't know what had hit him.

She gave him her most winning smile. "I'm here to talk about Lacy, of course."

Walker felt the curving of her lips to the very pit of his stomach but scowled anyway. "Of course." He folded his arms across his chest. "What is it about *my* daughter you feel compelled to discuss?"

"She's a lovely child. Very sweet. How do you take your coffee?"

"Black," he replied, narrowing his eyes.

She handed him his cup, using the opportunity to study him. His looks weren't standard or classic or pretty. He was tall and slim and had a serious, contemplative face. The kind of face women admired because it promised a wealth of sensitivity without losing a smidgen of strength, the kind of face women remembered. His dark-brown hair was almost curly, cut in a short conservative style that looked somehow boyish even though it shouldn't. His eyes were a nice brown—she'd noticed that right away—and topped by a slash of dark brows.

This morning those eyes were shadowed, his hair rumpled, cheeks unshaven. He had on a pair of old jeans, faded and worn until the fabric was thin, soft, and clung to him. His lightweight cotton sweater looked rumpled, as if he'd plucked it from a chair in haste; its vee exposed a glimpse of taut, tanned flesh.

He had the look of a man who had spent the night making love.

There was a fluttering at her pulse points, and Alex drew her eyebrows together. This wouldn't do, not at all. She refused to be attracted to him.

She held out the basket. "Muffin?"

Walker waved it aside. "Let's cut to the chase, shall we, Ms. Clare. Why are you here?"

Alex took a sip of her coffee. She had hoped to avoid a direct confrontation. It looked as if it wasn't to be. "I enjoyed meeting Lacy yesterday and when she expressed an interest in going on a crystal dig, I offered to take her. Later, I thought you might be concerned."

"Concerned?"

"Well, yes." She tried another of her "just little ole me" smiles. "I thought you might be concerned about a stranger issuing an invitation to your daughter. I came to reassure you."

"Go right ahead."

She laughed. "I thought I'd already started."

Walker found himself enjoying the sound of her laughter, wanting to laugh himself. But in this situation, he reminded himself, he wasn't a man, but a father.

"I can certainly see why you thought that," he said dryly. "You barge in with one of the Hounds of the Baskervilles and turn the place inside out."

She shook her head. "For some reason, harmless chaos seems to follow me. It drove my parents to distraction. Anyway"—she offered him the basket again—"I own a crystal and mineral shop here at Diamond Lakes and many of the quartz crystals I sell I dig myself. Normally I don't take people with me, but Lacy seemed lonely and it wouldn't be a problem. And I am harmless."

"That depends on your definition of harmless." Walker folded his arms across his chest. "Yesterday, you not only befriended my daughter but you also encouraged her to break several of my rules."

Alex tipped her head back, fighting off the beginnings of her temper. "Sometimes kids need to break a few, safe rules."

Walker counted to ten before he spoke. "Is that so? How many children do you have, Ms. Clare?"

"None, but I remember being one." She leaned forward earnestly. "I know you love Lacy—how could you not, she's wonderful. But a child can be smothered with love. She needs a little freedom, a chance to discover who she is. Do you understand what I'm saying?"

"I understand exactly what you're saying," Walker said stiffly as he stood and moved to the door. "Thank you for your concern. But Lacy and I are doing just fine."

Alex stood, but instead of heading toward the door, as he was silently suggesting, she faced him. "I don't know if you'll understand this, but I saw myself in Lacy. Myself as a child. A lonely child in need of a friend, in need of someone to understand."

"I don't like what you're suggesting."

"I'm not suggesting anything. I'm only—"

"Only telling me how to raise Lacy? Only insinuating that I'm not giving Lacy what she needs? That's pretty damn arrogant of someone who doesn't know the first thing about us or our situation. The subject is closed, Ms. Clare."

She looked at him furiously. For years she'd been told when to speak and what to say. She'd walked the path she'd been told to even when she'd known it was the wrong one. No more. She wouldn't back down from what she believed in or what she knew was right. "I know something's wrong with Lacy; I want to help her."

He was furious. She could see it in his eyes, in the tightening of his jaw. She could also see that he was trying to control himself. She'd gone too far.

"I think it'd be best for everyone if you left my daughter alone."

Heat crept up her cheeks. Heat born of anger, not embarrassment. "It wouldn't be best for Lacy," she said quietly.

He narrowed his eyes. Lacy would not be the victim of an irresponsible, selfish woman. Not again. He would make sure of that. "How do you know something's wrong with Lacy?" he demanded, his tone harsh. "Are you a psychic? A fortune teller? And how do you think you're going to help her? With baked goods?"

Alex slipped her trembling hands into the front pockets of her shorts. What would he say if she told him the truth—that she was an empath and that she might be able to help heal Lacy if he would let her? He would probably toss her out the door.

And maybe that would be for the best, she thought, a thread of doubt—and fear—worming through her. She had tried. She could walk away with a clear conscience. Then she heard the care-free sound of Lacy's laughter, and she acknowledged the truth. A half-hearted attempt wouldn't give her a clear conscience.

Taking a deep breath, she tried another tack. "Have you ever heard of metaphysical healing?

When I lived in California, I took a couple of courses in it. They believe—"

"That disease is all in the mind," he interrupted. "That there's a magic cure for everything from being overweight to headaches to . . . cancer. Trendy, painless, and cost efficient." He lifted his brows. "I don't know why I bothered with all that education."

His voice was deliberately bland; the very absence of inflection was more cutting than sarcasm.

She narrowed her eyes, just a little. "You'd find that if you were a little less rigid in your thinking, you'd stop getting neck aches. The knee problems you have are caused by that same inflexibility and would be eliminated as well."

He stared at her for a moment, his hand going to the back of his neck. Then as if realizing what he was doing, he dropped it. "Cute. What did I do, rub my neck?"

"Not at all." She flashed him a brilliant smile, enjoying being right. "Take a healthy dose of understanding and tolerance and call me in the morning."

For a moment Walker said nothing. "You can believe any damn thing you want—as long as you don't involve my daughter. Is that understanding enough, Ms. Clare? Can we close this subject now?"

"Fine." She started toward the door then, deciding to give it one more try, stopped and touched his arm. In that split second as their eyes met, she registered the heat of his flesh, the strength of his muscles, and something else. Something intimate and between only the two of them. If it were a sound it would be hushed, even throaty;

if a smell, that of a tropical flower, rare and pungent. Instead, it was a feeling, and it rippled lazily over her nerve endings until she felt vulnerable and afraid.

She dropped her hand and drew in a deep breath. The sound was ragged, and she hoped he hadn't noticed. "I'd still like to take Lacy on a crystal dig."

"I don't think so," he said his voice silky—and unsettling.

She tipped up her chin, meeting his eyes evenly. "She'll be disappointed."

"Yes, but children often don't know what's best for them."

"Nor do their parents."

They stared at each other for a long moment. Finally, softly, he said, "My daughter is needy and because of that, easily hurt. I'm asking you to leave her alone; I expect you to respect my wishes. If you don't, there'll be trouble."

There was nothing left for her to say, so she turned and walked out of the cottage, calling for Heinz as she did. Aware of his eyes on her back, she waved good-bye to Lacy and crossed the lawn.

Sighing, Alex selected a piece of rose quartz from the basket in front of her, then measured out enough silver wire to make it into a pendant. For the past two days she hadn't been able to concentrate on her work . . . or stop thinking about her confrontation with Walker Ridgeman. She also hadn't been able to forget the way she had felt when she'd touched him—aware and womanly and somehow connected to him.

Alex shook her head. The man that had caused

her pulse to race was an illusion, she reasoned, and had nothing to do with this society doctor from Boston. The other morning he had been rumpled and sleepy and off guard; she was crazy about his daughter. Surely that was a powerful influence on how she felt about—

The bell over the shop's door tinkled, interrupting her thoughts. Alex looked up, grateful for the distraction. When she saw who it was, she arched her brows in surprise. "Lacy, what are you doing here?"

The girl stopped just inside the door, her expression stricken. "You said I could . . . I mean, I thought . . ."

"Oh, Lacy, of course I'm delighted you're here! You caught me off guard, that's all. Welcome to Crystal Clare's. Then, almost as an afterthought, she asked, Does your father know you're here?"

"I asked him if I could come," Lacy murmured, a delicate pink easing up her cheeks. "Is this a . . . bad time?"

"Not at all." Alex smiled. "Actually, it's been quiet today. I've been using the time to make some jewelry. Would you like to see?"

"You make jewelry? Really?"

"Uh-huh. Over here." As Alex led Lacy to her small worktable at the back of the store, she slid the girl a questioning glance. Walker Ridgeman had been adamant that Alex's path not cross his daughter's. Somehow she doubted he had changed his mind so soon. But looking at Lacy's eager and open face now, she really didn't give a hoot what he thought. If Lacy said she'd asked permission, she had.

Alex pulled up a second stool beside the table and motioned for Lacy to sit down. "I don't do anything too fancy here, just some wire wrapping to make pendants. For the more elaborate pieces, I buy from real designers."

Lacy reached out and touched one of the wrapped stones. "This looks fancy to me."

"Trust me, it's not." Alex looked at the cluttered assortment of crystals in various sizes and colors on the table. "Do you still have your crystal?"

Lacy nodded, blushing again. "I take it everywhere. Even to bed."

"Good," Alex said softly, touched by the girl's openness. Her father had been right, Lacy was extremely vulnerable. "Would you like me to put it on a chain for you?"

Lacy caught her lower lip between her teeth, obviously torn.

Seeing the girl's battle, Alex added, "Of course I couldn't do it for free. It would cost . . . say"— she glanced at Lacy—"I'd have to charge you a dollar and a half. Do you have that much?"

"I think so." Lacy dug in her pocket and pulled out two singles. "I do!"

Smiling, Alex took the crystal from the girl's hand, her own fingers closing around it. A light shudder ran through her as she absorbed Lacy's energy from the stone. It passed quickly, and a moment later she met the girl's eyes. "All I do is take this light-gauge silver wire and wrap it around the crystal." She demonstrated. "You have to be sure to tuck the end under and around so it won't scratch you or snag your clothing. I make a loop for a chain . . ." several seconds passed as she worked with the wire and pliers ". . . and presto, a pendant."

Lacy rested her chin on her fist, her eyes wide

as she watched. "You make everything look so easy."

"Everything *is* easy, Lacy," she said, smiling. "It's all a matter of attitude. Now, choose a chain." When the girl had done that, Alex laced it through the loop for her, then slipped it over her head.

Lacy ran the delicate silver through her fingers. "It's really pretty, Alex. Thanks."

"You look great. Hold on, there's a mirror on the jewelry counter; I'll get it." Alex brought the mirror over and held it out so the girl could see for herself.

Lacy inspected the necklace for several moments, then looked shyly at Alex. "I've never met anyone like you before. You're so beautiful and so . . ." She shrugged and shifted her gaze, embarrassed. "I wish I looked like you."

"Thanks." Alex reached out and touched the girl's hair. "But you shouldn't wish to be anything but what you are. You're beautiful, Lacy. Look." She turned the mirror so Lacy's face was reflected in it. Lacy blushed and averted her eyes, and Alex's heart wrenched. She remembered another little girl, a child who had always wished to be something other than what she was, a child who had desperately tried to fit into a mold that had been all wrong.

Alex touched Lacy's hair again. "We're all beautiful. It's what's on the inside shining out that determines beauty. You *are* beautiful on the outside, Lacy. But even better, you're beautiful on the inside too."

Lacy took a peek at her reflection, then turned to Alex. "You really think so?"

Alex silently swore as she read gratitude, and

doubt, in the girl's eyes. Somebody had done a number on this child, and she was certain it played a large part in her problem. "Yes, I really do. Now"—she let out a quick breath and stood—"I promised you a tour. Shall we?"

For the next fifteen minutes, Alex led Lacy around the shop, explaining the difference between pink, smoky, and citrine quartz, discussing the various shades, from light to deep violet, of amethyst, and letting Lacy hold any crystal or mineral that caught her eye, including ones shaped into spheres, eggs, and pyramids.

"This one's neat." Lacy picked up a large crystal with a point on both ends. Her eyes widened. "My whole arm's tingling."

Alex smiled and joined her. "That's one of the finest pieces in the shop. It's called a double terminator because of the two points. Here, look at this—"

"Dad!"

Alex looked up. Walker Ridgeman stood in the doorway looking as if he could do murder.

Uneasily, Alex glanced from the father's furious face to the daughter's stricken one. Her earlier suspicion had been correct: Lacy had not gotten permission to visit.

Alex reached out to put a reassuring hand on Lacy's arm but touched only air. The girl slid to the floor, catching the edge of the card table on her way down. Lacy's head hit the wood floor with a thud that made Alex's heart skip a beat.

Before she could even bend down to help the girl, Walker was across the room and kneeling by her side, gently stroking her face. "It's all right, Muffin," he crooned. "Shh . . . everything's fine. You're fine."

"Is there anything I can do?" Alex asked. "Anything I can get—"

"Leave her alone," he snapped. "Don't do anything. Just . . . leave . . . us alone."

Alex took a step back. In his eyes she read absolute panic and absolute love; generating in waves from his being were terror and fury. Fury not directed at her, but at someone else or everyone else—and at himself.

Lacy's lids fluttered. "D . . . Dad?"

Alex closed her eyes and breathed a silent sigh of relief. Even though Lacy's spell had lasted only a minute or two, it had felt much longer.

Lacy sat up unsteadily, pushing the hair out of her eyes. "I'm sorry, Dad. I—"

"Shh—" He helped her stand. "We'll discuss it when you feel better."

"But I feel fi—" She was on her feet then and saw the destruction on the floor. "Oh, no, Alex, your crystals! I've probably broken them all!"

"Don't worry." Alex smiled and made a small gesture with her fingers. "They've endured much worse than this little spill." She met Walker's eyes, attempting to silently tell him that his daughter could also endure more than a tumble to the floor.

He met her gaze, much of the emotion from earlier gone now. What was left tugged at her, and she folded her arms across her chest. She couldn't be drawn to this man. She absolutely could not.

Walker looked at his daughter. "We should go, Lacy."

The girl stopped at the door and looked back at her. "Thanks for the necklace."

"Don't thank me, you paid for it." Alex smiled at Lacy, then tossed a defiant glance at her father.

Walker held her gaze for a second more, then let the door snap shut behind them.

The afternoon business was as slow as the morning's had been, and Alex had too much time to think about Lacy's frightening tumble. One moment she had been fine, the next she'd been out cold. It had been obvious from the way they'd both acted that this wasn't the first time she'd had that type of a spell. It had also been obvious that Lacy had handled whatever it was better than her father.

Alex drew her brows together as her thoughts drifted to Walker. He'd been beside himself with fear . . . and guilt. There was a flutter deep inside her as she remembered the tone of his voice as he'd stroked his daughter's cheek—soft and gentle and vulnerable, the flutter became a ripple as she remembered the look in his eyes the moment before he and Lacy had walked out the door.

Alex realized what she was doing and straightened up, annoyed with herself. With a toss of her head, she tried to push him from her thoughts— she was as unsuccessful this time as she'd been all afternoon.

Frowning, she crossed to the cash register to begin closing out. Dr. Walker Ridgeman was as wrong for her as a person could be, she told herself. She took the ones from the drawer, counted them out, made a notation, then began with the fives. She only felt this connection with him because of her involvement with Lacy. Sure. How many times had she thought she felt something for one of her patients, when in reality it had been the empathy?

This was different, Alex admitted. She'd never felt a sexual pull before. And this was definitely that. She stared blankly at the bills in her hand, then began to count them again.

But how could that be? How could she feel attracted to a man who was arrogant and opinionated and uptight?

She wasn't. It was his softness with Lacy that drew her, his vulnerability.

Alex realized she'd lost count again, muttered a curt word under her breath, and stuffed the money back into the drawer. She would count it in the morning.

On edge and eager to go home, Alex shut off the lights and turned over the "open" sign in the window. Just then the phone rang. She thought about ignoring it, then on a whim, picked it up.

It was Walker Ridgeman.

"What can I do for you?" she asked, working to keep hesitation out of her voice. She didn't feel up to another confrontation right now.

"Can we meet? I'd like to talk to you . . . about Lacy."

Alex curled her fingers around the phone cord, her heartbeat quickening. "When and where?"

"Eight o'clock, the Gazebo bar."

"I'll see you then." Without another word, Alex placed the receiver back in its cradle. Drawing a deep breath, she sagged against the counter and willed her runaway heart to slow. She should have refused. She was too susceptible tonight; she was losing her objectivity. Alex bit back a laugh. What a joke. She'd lost her objectivity the same moment she'd become totally involved; it was too late to turn back.

But she could still play it safe, could still keep some distance between herself and Walker Ridgeman. Exhaling her breath in a determined rush, she let herself out of the shop.

Three

Walker took a seat at the Gazebo Bar, ordered a Bombay and tonic, then checked his watch. He was twenty minutes early, just as he'd planned. He had wanted to watch her arrive.

He drummed his fingers against the tile bar, his eyes trained on the entrance. This afternoon had shaken him. Badly. Lacy had never disobeyed him before, even when she'd professed to want something "more than anything." But today she had. And it had been to see a woman she barely knew.

But worse, much worse, she'd had one of her spells. Walker dragged a hand through his dark hair, guilt eating at him. If only he hadn't been so hard-nosed, if only he'd paid more attention to what she'd been saying.

And the past few days, everything Lacy had said seemed to have something to do with Alex or the crystal she clutched to her as if it was the most precious thing on earth. Walker grimaced. She had begged him to allow her to visit the woman.

His chest tightened at the truth—he'd forced her to choose, and she had chosen Alex.

He took a deep, steadying breath and told himself to be logical. Lacy hadn't chosen one over the other, she'd considered her options and made a decision. Her action hadn't been so much one of defiance as of deliberation. She was ten now and fast approaching adolescence. And with adolescence came the desire for independence.

There was a catch in his chest and Walker swallowed hard, dragging his thoughts away from Lacy's approaching independence. Looking at it rationally, her fascination with Alex Clare wasn't hard to understand. Lacy's own mother had paid so little attention to her that now she was hungry for a woman's, any woman's, interest. And Alex was so unlike the other women in Lacy's experience, including her mother, that she felt safe, or like himself, intrigued.

Walker narrowed his eyes. There, he'd admitted it. Alex Clare intrigued him. That was part of the reason he was here tonight, it was why he had arrived early. He was a man of reason, of convention, and he couldn't help but wonder what made a woman like her tick.

The bartender served his drink then, and in the moment he turned to the man, he almost missed what he'd made such haste to see. Although, Walker thought, watching her cross the patio, he didn't know how he could have. Alex Clare had the kind of looks that were unmissable and, in a strange way, unforgettable. It was more than her fiery mane of hair, more than the odd mix of colors and patterns she put together and wore with such panache.

He stood and pulled out her chair as she

approached the table. Most women would have worn a dress or something equally feminine, even revealing. Not her. She had on a shorts-suit. The knee length shorts and matching long jacket were both an olive green-and-black check and made from a soft, wrinkled cotton. The tank top she wore underneath was a brilliant fuchsia color that should have clashed with either the olive or her hair but didn't. On her feet were a pair of flat sandals that tied around the ankles.

He shook his head as she slid into the chair.

She smiled up at him in acknowledgment of his gesture, then waited to speak until he had reseated himself. "I see you're also a habitual early bird."

"Not usually."

Walker saw the question in her eyes, the way her eyebrows lifted just a little, but ignored both. He had her slightly off-balance and wasn't about to give up his advantage just yet.

"Your call surprised me," she said.

"I'll bet." He signaled to the waiter. "What would you like to drink?"

"Cranberry juice, please."

"First bran muffins, now cranberry juice. You must be one of those healthy types."

"*Homemade* bran muffins," she teased, "and yes, I guess you could call me that."

"You don't mind that I have something stronger?"

"Not at all."

The waiter arrived and Walker ordered the juice, then turned back to her. "Now I'm surprised. I would have thought you'd be more opinionated than that. Or would have at least given me a lecture."

"Why?" She ran a finger along the delicate silver

chain at her throat, her lips curving. "Do you think I'm some sort of zealot?" His look told her he did and she laughed. "Actually I'm quite the opposite."

Walker followed the movement of her fingers as she toyed with the necklace, he couldn't find the willpower to look away. "Really?"

The juice arrived and for a moment they were silent. After she'd sipped, she looked back at him. "What about you, Dr. Ridgeman? Projecting your quirks onto other people?"

The corners of his lips lifted in amusement. "I'm not opinionated, Ms. Clare. I'm always right."

She laughed again, charmed. When he smiled like that he looked about twenty and positively irresistible. "That would be pretty scary if I thought you meant it."

"What makes you think I don't?"

"We're here aren't we? That seems an admission of sorts."

"You have a point." Walker lifted his glass then set it back down without sipping. In the last few minutes his curiosity, instead of being satisfied, had grown. Alex Clare was a woman of contrasts: She had the hair of a seductress and the personality of a pixie, dressed California casual but carried herself like Boston old money and, he was discovering, her wit could be as sharp as her smile was soft.

Alex met his gaze evenly. "There's a question in your eyes, go ahead and ask it."

"All right," Walker said, "I can't figure you out. You don't seem to fit."

She brushed the hair away from her face, pleased. Ten years ago that statement would have sent her into a panic. "And my fitting into a nice, neat mold is important to you?"

"I like order. I like things to make sense."

Alex thought of her parents and one corner of her mouth lifted in wry amusement. She understood him better than he ever would have guessed. "What's the problem?" she held out her hands, palms up. "What is it about this picture that doesn't work?"

Walker lifted his drink. "I just need a few more facts, that's all."

"The Sherlock Holmes approach," she said, lightly. "Find and study all the clues, then solve the mystery. Logical, orderly, clean. Predictable, Dr. Ridgeman."

"And how would you solve a mystery?"

"Gut reaction," she said simply, gesturing with her glass. "Instinct."

He smiled. "You've just given me a clue."

"So I have."

They laughed together, then were silent for several moments. When she met his eyes once again, he said, "You're not from Arkansas. You have a southern accent, but it's different. Softer at the edges."

"You're right." Her hand went once again to the silver chain at her throat. "I'm from Atlanta."

"Atlanta," he repeated. "Why did you choose here? Why rocks?"

He has nice hands, she thought, watching him as he trailed his index finger along the side of his glass. Her heart began to beat a little faster, and she looked away. "I've always loved rocks, always loved digging for them. My parents bought me fancy dolls, but I preferred mud and a shovel."

Imagining this woman in ruffles and playing with dolls brought a smile to his lips. "So you came here with the idea of starting a business."

"Heavens no, I came here by mistake. I was tired and discouraged and had heard about Hot Springs and Crystal Mountain. I fell in love and stayed."

Walker tightened his fingers on his glass. "Is he still around?"

"Who?"

"The guy."

Alex shook her head. "Not a guy. I fell in love with this place."

Walker let out a long breath. "I see. What did your family think of your decision?"

"My parents hate what I do," she said. "They think this is no way for any woman to live, let alone a Stanton Clare."

She'd said the last lightly, almost too lightly. She would be furious with herself if she knew how much that told him about her. "Any brothers or sisters?"

Alex lowered her eyes. "A brother. A terribly conventional and successful engineer."

"It really makes you mad, doesn't it."

Alex looked at him, surprised. She found her lips tipping up at the corners. "I have a redheaded temper, no doubt about it. I call it my whizzer. But don't worry, you have to really push me before I lose it."

Walker laughed, loudly and honestly. It occurred to him that he'd laughed too little of late. It also occurred to him that he found her too attractive. "I'll remember that."

"You'd do well to. Once I . . ." Her words faltered as she realized Walker's eyes were no longer fixed on hers. He had lowered them to a point somewhere below her chin. Her flesh heated under his gaze, and she shifted her seat.

He leaned across the table and with his right

forefinger only, hooked the fine silver chain that hung around her neck. It was the single piece of jewelry she wore; attached to it and nestled between her breasts was a clear quartz crystal set in silver. "Your hand goes to this often. Did you know that?"

Alex caught her breath, a small shudder moving through her as his finger brushed against her collarbone, then lower. The delicate metal skimmed slowly over her flesh, a moment later he had the crystal. Alex released her pent-up breath in a small rush, then drew another.

Walker's fingers closed around the stone. It seemed to tingle against his fingers, and he met her eyes. "Tell me about this."

"It's a quartz crystal."

"I know that."

"Oh."

He rubbed the stone between his fingers. It was warm from her body. "Some people consider quartz crystals magical. Is that why you wear it?"

Alex took a deep shaky breath. "I find it very beautiful."

"Very beautiful," Walker said, his voice thick. "Is that all? No magic? Nothing for me to be skeptical of?"

"You'll think it's ridiculous."

He leaned closer. "Try me."

He was so near she could feel his breath against her skin, and her pulse raced. She cleared her throat once again. "There are people who believe crystals have the ability, because they're conductors of energy, to help balance, even heal, the person wearing them."

Walker lifted his eyes from the crystal to hers. "And why do you wear it, Alexis Stanton Clare? Because of their beauty or because of their magic?"

At the look in his eyes, her heart skipped a beat. There was amusement there, and challenge. A challenge that involved more than agile wits and a sharp tongue. His was elemental, physical. And he would, she knew, play to win.

Alex pulled back slightly, and the crystal slipped from his fingers and back between her breasts. His heat, his energy, lingered on the stone and she felt it to the very center of her being. She steeled herself against the sensation. "I thought we were here to talk about Lacy."

Walker was silent for a long moment. Finally, softly, he said, "So we are." He signed the check and stood, holding out a hand to help her up, "I thought we could walk."

Alex gazed up at him. For all his guards, there was a hint of vulnerability in his eyes, a trace of pain. She felt both as if they were her own. Without another word, she took his hand and stood. Together they exited the bar and headed down the path that led to the duck pond.

The walkway that circled the pond was brick and lined with lanterns, the surrounding trees were laced in tiny white lights. They walked without speaking. Except for the splash of water from one of the fountains and an occasional complaint from a disgruntled duck, it was quiet.

They passed another couple who were arm in arm and obviously in love, and Alex swallowed past the lump that formed in her throat. She slid a glance at Walker's strong profile, suddenly aware of each brush of his arm against hers, of the unhurried cadence of his breathing and of the way he fitted his longer stride to her shorter one.

She frowned as she thought of how other things would fit—things like mouths and hands.

Images followed, and she gave her head a small shake. It was a magical, romantic night and she was succumbing to the soft breeze and velvety sky, she told herself. Her quivering nerve endings and wayward thoughts had more to do with not having taken a moonlight stroll with a man in ages than with the man himself.

They stopped on an arched footbridge and looked down at the water. Two mallards swam beneath the bridge, creating a gentle wake behind them. Seconds ticked past. Finally Alex turned toward him. "Why have you changed your mind?"

Walker met her eyes. "I haven't."

"Then why are we here?"

"Because," he answered slowly, "I love my daughter more than anything else on earth, and for some reason she wants to be with you." He curled his fingers around the smooth wooden railing. "I saw today that you make her happy. That's something she isn't often enough."

"Oh, Walker." His name passed her lips as if she'd been born saying it, as if it belonged there. Without questioning the feeling, Alex laid her hand over his. It was as warm and strong as a man's should be, but there was something of the child in the way his fingers closed around hers. When he turned to her, all her pulse points fluttered in unison, and her knees turned to pudding.

She should be smart, she told herself. Pull away from him, run even. Instead she tightened her fingers. There would be plenty of time to deal with what she should and shouldn't be feeling, tomorrow was soon enough for warnings and recriminations. Now was for the moment . . . she leaned toward him.

Walker's breath caught. Her hand over his was

meant to reassure, to comfort. Instead it awakened, excited. How long had it been since he'd wanted to hold a woman? Walker wondered, gazing into her clear green eyes. Oh sure, he'd wanted sex, but not softness, had wanted passion, but not promise. And now, at this moment, he felt as if he wanted it all—the promises, the softness . . . and even the regrets.

Walker lowered his eyes to her mouth. It was rose hued and trembled slightly. The urge to taste that mouth, to have it heat and part under his washed over him so suddenly it took his breath away. Even as he bent his head, he thought of Lacy. He couldn't afford to want this woman, couldn't afford to put aside good sense for an evening, or even a moment. He jerked his gaze away from her tempting mouth and straightened.

Her disappointment stunned her. She'd wanted his kiss more than she'd ever wanted a kiss before, more than she could have thought possible. Alex lifted her eyes to his hard profile. Their hands still touched, but the connection was broken—his felt stiff and unyielding under hers.

"Walker?" she asked, her voice sounding husky even to her own ears.

Several seconds ticked past, then finally, almost without emotion, he said, "This afternoon Lacy had a cataplexic spell."

He was going to pretend nothing had just happened between them, Alex realized. No magic, no connection, nothing. She slipped her hand from his denying that she felt hurt.

"A cataplexic spell is a momentary paralysis brought on by sudden emotional reactions, good or bad," he continued without prompting. "This afternoon . . . I startled her. She knew she'd disobeyed me and"—he cleared his throat—"I've never been the cause of one of her spells before."

His voice was tight, strained. She felt his distress, his guilt, but resisted the urge to reach out and touch him again. "You're her father, Walker. Fathers are supposed to make rules and expect their children to obey them. You didn't do anything wrong."

"Didn't I? Sometimes I think I did everything wrong," he said softly. "About a year ago Lacy was diagnosed as having narcolepsy."

"The sleep disorder," Alex murmured in surprise, thinking of the pains she'd felt in her throat and chest. That was odd.

"You've heard of it, then. I'm surprised; it's relatively rare."

"I don't know much about it other than its sufferers fall asleep a lot."

"There are other symptoms: hallucinatory dreams, sleep paralysis, and . . . what you witnessed today." Walker looked up at the sky, then at her. "So you were right," he said stiffly. "There is something wrong with Lacy."

"Being right isn't important to me."

He stared at her a moment, than started walking again. This time he moved faster, and Alex had to work to keep up. He stopped after a few feet and turned back toward her. "We need to set some ground rules."

"Oh?" She held onto her temper, telling herself he was hurting. "What did you have in mind?"

"You can see Lacy as long as you promise there'll be no talk of metaphysical cures and magic stones. In other words, no mumbo jumbo. I'll tag along just to be sure."

Alex stiffened her spine. She was angry. There

was no pretending, no talking herself out of it. He was arrogant, opinionated and shortsighted. "Why do you feel so threatened by me?"

"The only one who I feel is threatened is Lacy. We came here to become accustomed to her disease. Once she's comfortable—"

"That's exactly what you don't want to do!" Alex swept her hair away from her face. "She'll never be well then."

"Don't you get it? There's no cure for narcolepsy. No known cause, no cure, end of story."

"Metaphysical healers believe that negative thought patterns are the cause of disease and conversely, that changing those patterns is the cure for them. What do you have to lose? You already said there's nothing the medical profession can—"

"Enough! This conversation is over."

When he tried to turn away from her, Alex grabbed his arm. For too many years she'd bitten her tongue and tried to play it other people's way—she wasn't about to do it again, and certainly not for him! "Why is Lacy so insecure? She's a beautiful girl, but today she wouldn't even look in a mirror. She's hurting so badly, why won't you let me—"

"Offer her a placebo? No thanks, we'll do without that this week." He shook off her hand. "You have a choice—my conditions or nothing."

She wanted to help Lacy and knew she could. But she wasn't about to let this unenlightened Neanderthal order her around. "It seems to me," she said with deceptive softness, "that I should be the one setting the ground rules. *Your* daughter wants to spend time with me. I like her and would enjoy that, but I'm not about to abide by your silly rules."

Alex realized her hands were trembling. "Lacy expressed an interest in digging for crystals; I've got a trip planned tomorrow. Now, *you* take it or leave it."

Walker stared at her a moment, his mouth pulled into a hard line. "Fine," he finally said. "Just tell me when and where."

"Morning is best, so let's try to leave by eight. I'll drop off directions to my place at the concierge's. Dress appropriately." Without waiting for him to respond or follow, she started back the way they'd come.

Alex leaned on her porch railing and drew in a lungful of the morning air. It was cool and crisp with a tang of fall belied by the day's projected high of eighty-eight. She released her pent-up breath, smiled, and stretched. She felt as fresh, as rejuvenated as the new day.

Which after her fury of last night was as much of a relief as a surprise. Alex combed her fingers through her sleep-tumbled hair, then dropped her hands to the railing once again. It had taken two hours of rationalizing to herself and countless cups of chamomile tea to calm down.

She'd lost her whizzer, no doubt about it.

From behind her she heard Heinz's tail thump against the floor. She patted her leg and he came over to her. "You're good company, Heinz," she said, scratching behind his ears. "You don't talk back, you don't criticize, and you don't try to make me into something I'm not." He paid her back with a slobbery kiss, then ambled off the porch in search of an even better place to snooze.

Alex watched him go, a frown creasing her brow. She hadn't been that angry in a long time. She pursed her lips, thinking back. Not since her mother's last call, two-and-a-half months ago.

She shook her head. What was it about Walker that could draw her temper out that way? Few people—excluding her parents—had ever had the ability to do that, and certainly not so quickly.

It hadn't been his criticism of her beliefs, at least it shouldn't have been. Years ago she'd adopted the policy that if someone had a problem with what she believed or did, she walked away. She'd lived by that policy.

Until now. Until Walker.

Why? Alex frowned, acknowledging the truth. She'd been angry because it *had* mattered to her what he thought. She sighed. And because he hadn't wanted to kiss her when she'd been dying to kiss him.

As the thought registered, she straightened. Nonsense! Foolish feminine pride had never been one of her shortcomings; she'd never been a person who thought in terms of revenge or jealousy. And as for caring what he thought, for some perverse reason she was attracted to Walker Ridgeman. But that didn't mean his opinion mattered to her on a level that could wound or excite. And it most definitely wasn't something she couldn't handle.

From now on she would smile and laugh, she would keep it light and fun. And if she found herself feeling drawn to him, she would remind herself that he was the kind of man who liked nice, neat packages, packages that made sense.

That settled, she called out to Heinz, then headed inside to dress.

Walker took one last glance at his sleeping daughter and climbed out of the car. As promised, Alex had left the directions to her place with the resort's concierge. They'd been good ones, and he hadn't had difficulty finding the cabin even though it was located on an unnamed dirt road at the edge of the Ouachita National Forest. Setting his jaw, Walker started across the drive—if you could call it that—and climbed the two uneven steps to the porch. He didn't like being coerced. Nor did he like being outmaneuvered. Alex Clare had done both—and without even breaking a sweat. The truth of that didn't improve his mood.

As he stepped up onto the porch, he heard Heinz bark. Walker arched his brows. For such a huge beast, the dog's bark was high and almost whiny—like a poodle or some other pint-sized pup. Just another thing attached to Alex that didn't quite fit.

Alex opened the door before he had a chance to knock. She was wearing a pair of faded blue jeans and a red T-shirt that boldly proclaimed *Miracles Happen* while a wide-brim straw hat dangled from her left hand. Her unruly hair had been somewhat tamed by pulling it into a single braid down her back. Her face was devoid of cosmetics. She looked naive and natural and about as different from the women he found attractive as humanly possible. He silently swore. "Ready?"

Alex smiled brightly. "Well, good morning to you too." She swung the door wider and peered around him. "Where's Lacy?"

"In the car. Mornings aren't her best time."

Her smile faded. "You should have told me. We could have done this later—"

Walker lifted his hand. "It's the unexpected sleep attacks that are hard to deal with. This is fine. She'll just be in and out of sleep for the next hour or so."

"Perfect, that's about how long we'll be on the road." She stepped aside. "Come in. I'm not quite ready."

Her smile was small and subtly sassy; it hit him with the force of a freight train at full speed. He cleared his throat, frowning against the sensations she'd caused. She was up to something. Smiling and laughing and acting like they were the best of friends didn't add up. After last night's confrontation, friendly had been the last thing he'd expected.

Walker followed her inside, almost tripping over Heinz as he did.

She was turned the other way, humming under her breath as she gathered together an odd assortment of paraphernalia. As he watched, she bent over to retrieve a basket. He followed the movement with his eyes, his pulse accelerating. He caught himself and muttered a curt word. Maybe he should be less concerned with what she was up to and more concerned with his own behavior. He was acting like he hadn't been alone with a beautiful woman since he'd hit puberty.

His gaze lingered even as he reminded himself that he was here to see that Alex Clare didn't fill his daughter's head with unrealistic—and ultimately harmful—notions. The last thing he should be doing is noticing the womanly curve of her hips or the way the faded denim of her jeans molded to those curves.

"I packed a lunch and a couple of thermoses," Alex said, straightening. "There's no place to get anything up there."

"You didn't have to do that," he said, forcibly turning his attention from her to her home. The cabin consisted of one room and a loft, and was sparsely furnished with a mishmash of early attic furniture. He wished he could find something about it to criticize, but there was nothing. It was rustic, simple and, surprisingly, charming.

"Well, I am the group leader today. Besides"— she looked up from the wicker basket and grinned—"you might not want to thank me until you see the fare. No meat, potato chips, or sodas."

Walker met her gaze. Why hadn't he noticed before that her eyebrows and lashes were the same daring red as the hair on her head? And how had he ever been idiot enough to wonder if the color was from a bottle?

"Today," she continued, laughing, "you rough it, Doc."

He found himself returning her teasing smile. "Just tell me there's no tofu and I'll suffer my fate in silence."

"There's no tofu."

Still smiling, they stared at each other until Walker realized what he was doing and jerked his gaze away. Annoyed, he crossed to one of the cabin's many windows. They were all thrown wide to invite in both the morning sun and breezes. Each ledge was lined with crystals in many different configurations, sizes, and colors.

"Crystals like the sun," she said from behind him.

"Pardon?"

"Like all other forms of life, crystals thrive in the sun."

Her eyes were laughing, but he suspected she was serious. "You talk about them as if they were alive."

"Do I?"

"Yes, you do."

A faint smile touched her mouth. "I'll have to watch that," she said, lightly. "So, what do you think of my place?"

"It suits you."

She laughed. "I considered myself really lucky to find it, furniture and all. When I decided I wanted to stay in Hot Springs, I didn't have anything but a weekend's worth of clothes and forty-four dollars."

"Dad?"

Walker turned at the sound of his daughter's voice, questions forgotten. Lacy was standing in the doorway, rubbing her eyes. He held out his arm. "Hi, Muffin, how are you feeling?"

"Okay." She yawned as she crossed the room. She stepped into the protective curve of his arm and looked at him, then at Alex. "I don't want to sleep anymore, I'll miss everything!" The dog's tail thumped against the floor as if in affirmation of her words. "Even Heinz thinks so!"

Alex laughed and touched her on the arm. "I promise you won't miss a thing. Now," she said in a no-nonsense tone of voice, "let's do something about your hair."

"My hair?" Lacy shot her father a worried glance. "Like what?"

"Like a braid." Laughing again, Alex put her hands on Lacy's shoulders and steered her toward a stool at the kitchen counter. "It's going to be hot up there. The mining company clears away all the trees before they begin digging into the mountain. Consequently there's no shade and usually little breeze. I have hats for all of us but this will get the hair off the back of your neck."

"Okay." Lacy plopped down on the stool, but didn't sit still, swiveling her head from right to left in her eagerness to see everything. "This is a neat place, Alex. Like something out of a movie. Someday I want one just like it."

Walker fought back an uncomfortable and unfamiliar twinge. Every time she looked at Alex her whole face lit up. Everything Alex had or said or did was better, more exciting than anything he could ever do or be. He shook his head. It wasn't jealousy he was feeling—not only jealousy anyway—it was fear. What would he do if he lost her?

While he watched, Alex pulled the brush slowly through Lacy's hair, then divided it into three sections and began plaiting. Her fingers worked quickly and she laughed and talked around the rubber band she held in her teeth. A catch formed in his chest. There was something warm and rosy and right about the scene he was witnessing.

And sensual, he thought, surprised. In the way a Mary Cassatt painting of mother and child was. Earthy and elemental and so soft it was like a whisper, so strong it was like the pull of the ocean. He could imagine the three of them spending Sunday mornings together. And rainy Saturdays, and evenings after dinner dishes were done.

He could imagine Alex in his bed.

Walker bit back an oath and dragged his gaze away. He was losing his mind.

Muttering something he hoped sounded like he was going to load the car, Walker snatched up the picnic basket and strode from the room.

Four

A few minutes later, Alex and Lacy stepped out onto the porch. "Oh, no," Alex murmured, looking at the car Walker had driven over in, the same car he had just finished loading—an immaculate Mercedes sedan.

"What's wrong?" Walker asked, turning toward her.

"Well . . ." she drew the word out, "the road up the mountain is rough even without the downpour we had last night, plus we're going to get pretty filthy. We'd be better off in my jeep—four-wheel drive and crummy."

When he was about to protest, Lacy clapped her hands in excitement. "Oh, boy, I've never ridden in a jeep before! Isn't it neat, Dad? A jeep!"

Alex swallowed a laugh as she watched the two of them shift everything from one vehicle to the other. Poor Walker, he was outmatched and outnumbered. The laugh sneaked out despite her attempt to hold it back.

When the two finished, Alex held up a lavender

and white striped sock filled with sulphur. "There's one more thing we have to do before we leave." She shook the sock, then sneezed. "To keep the chiggers away."

"Chiggers?" Lacy repeated, tentatively.

"It's a parasite that burrows just under the skin. It itches like crazy." Alex patted herself with the filled sock. That done, she crooked her finger for Lacy to come closer. After throwing an uneasy look at her father she did, and Alex dusted her with the contents of the sock.

"I know why it keeps 'em away," Lacy said, crinkling her nose in distaste. "It stinks."

"True, but the beauty of it is, we're all going to smell the same. Even Heinz." All three looked at the dog who had inched under the jeep and was whining. "Big baby," Alex scolded. She crossed over to him and dusted the end that was sticking out from under the jeep. "I'll get the rest of you later." She turned to Walker and held out the makeshift bag. "Dr. Ridgeman?"

"Go ahead, Dad, let Alex do it. After a minute it's not so bad."

"If you say so, Muffin." With a wicked grin, Walker stepped closer and held up his arms in an imitation of Lacy. "Ready when you are."

Heat crept up Alex's cheeks; she felt the red and cursed it. More than Lacy's innocent suggestion, it was what her own mind did with the suggestion that caused her blood pressure to sky-rocket—she imagined patting the bag over the muscular planes of his body, moving slowly, paying special attention to . . .

She eyed his mocking expression. He was laughing at her! His lips were turned up at the corners in a superior but sexy-as-hell smile. She jerked her gaze away. The man's mouth should come with an FDA warning: too potent for everyday exposure. And as for the rest of him, she thought with a sniff, she would make a point of keeping her eyes up and her mind on the day's excursion and the reason for it.

"I think your father can give himself the sock treatment," she said, tossing the sulphur bag at him with more force than necessary.

The sock hit him square in the chest, leaving a yellow mark on his blue chambray shirt. "Nice shot," Walker said, amused. He picked the bag up from the ground. "Let's see if I have the day's itinerary correct, Alex. We're going to bake in the sun, get filthy, and dodge parasites. To get to all this fun we have to take a bone-crunching, joint-jostling, hour-long ride to the middle of nowhere in your jeep."

Alex's cheeks heated as she realized that not only had she been watching the tap-tap of the bag as he dusted himself with the powder . . . she'd been watching it as if mesmerized. So much for keeping her eyes averted and her mind on business. She forced her gaze away for the second time in the space of five minutes, as annoyed with herself as him. "Personally, I think finding something that took thousands of years for the earth to make, something that is nearly perfect in its natural form even though its creation occurred under intense heat, pressure, and odds, is more than worth a few hours of discomfort—which, by the way, I happen not to find uncomfortable at all!"

Walker laughed then, and Alex realized she'd been had. She'd promised herself she would keep it light and friendly, that she would remain in control. Walker had turned the tables on her with one comment.

Angling her chin up, she stalked to the jeep and jerked open the door. Heinz eagerly jumped into the back seat. A grinning Lacy piled in behind him.

Just as Alex started to climb in, Walker touched her elbow. He glanced at his daughter to make sure she wouldn't hear, then met Alex's clear, green gaze. "You can drop the cheerful act," he murmured. "We're not friends, and we both know why I'm here."

Temper threaded through her; she held onto it. He could handle her anger or indignation, she knew. He would even welcome them. But she wasn't about to make it easy for him. She smiled sweetly. "Act? I don't know what you mean. I'm just being myself." Without waiting for his reply, she slipped behind the wheel and started the car.

Alex and Walker didn't speak again for some time. Although the trip passed quietly, it wasn't uneventful. After only a few miles, Alex got her first glimpse of one of Lacy's sleep attacks. One minute the child was wide awake and chattering, the next she had sagged against Heinz and was sound asleep. She had simply, and without warning, nodded off.

And just as simply a moment later, she awakened and picked up her thoughts where she had left off.

Alex cut Walker an astounded glance. He met her gaze without comment, but she read both frustration and resignation in his eyes. And she felt pain—the pain of a father for a daughter, of a man for himself. She sucked in a deep breath to steady herself as the sensations moved through her.

A moment later the feelings passed, and Alex released her pent-up breath. Only then did she realize she'd felt Walker's pain, not Lacy's.

The knowledge shook her, just a little, and she clenched the steering wheel. *She was not becoming involved with this man,* she told herself, *she would not "connect" with him.* She had to protect herself.

"We have the perfect day because of last night's rain," she said, suddenly needing to fill the quiet. She spoke loud enough to be heard over the wind rushing in the windows. "You'll see what I mean when we get there."

Lacy leaned forward eagerly. "What will we find, Alex? Will there be lots?"

Alex smiled at the girl in the rearview mirror. Lacy's expression was rapt. "At this mine all we'll find is clear quartz crystals—like the one I gave you. But there are clusters—groups of crystals stuck together—as well as the single crystals. There's also an infinite range of clarity and sizes within the crystals as well as single and double terminators, or points. And yes, there'll be lots."

Alex downshifted as she started up an incline. "It'll be hard to see how good a piece you've found until we've cleaned them. They'll be coated with iron oxide from the red clay earth. We'll take care of that later."

"How do we get down into the mine?" Lacy was practically squirming in her seat now. "Do we take an elevator?"

"Bad news, kiddo, this is open-pit mining—we don't go underground. The mining company comes in with bulldozers and digs into the side of the mountain. They extract and haul away as much as they can, but there will be piles of earth—some as high as ten or fifteen feet—for us to go through. Also, this company lets individuals go into the pit itself. There we can dig into the walls or scavenge through the debris on the floor of the pit."

"Oh."

At her crestfallen look, Alex added. "Check the bag in back. I have hats for all of us, pick the one you want." Lacy pulled out one with a huge orange flower attached to the brim. "I like this one!"

"Too bad," Alex teased. "I thought that one would be perfect for your dad.

Lacy giggled, Walker muttered something about women, and Alex chalked one up for the home team.

The rest of the trip passed as quietly as the beginning had. Lacy nodded off several times but neither Alex or Walker commented on that fact. They followed the curving road as it gave way to gently rolling hills. The area was sparsely populated. They passed nothing more than an occasional motel or restaurant. Alex made only one stop before the actual pit site—the mining company where she paid a fee for the three of them to dig.

As they pulled up to the pit, Alex released her breath in a long sigh. The rain had washed away enough of the earth to expose hundreds of crystals; they poked out of the side of the pit, blinking and twinkling in the sun like a wall of diamonds. She'd known what to expect—she'd seen this phenomenon dozens of times before—yet she was as

awed as the first time. She glanced at Walker—
even he looked startled by the beauty of it.

The three of them climbed from the jeep and
Alex passed out the equipment they would need—
screwdrivers and small garden tools to gently
move the earth away. As she did, she explained
rock ethics. "Don't try to force a crystal, if it's
ready to be taken from the earth, it will just
loosen into your hand. If a quartz is attached to
a cluster that won't loosen, don't break it off. It
sounds funny, but if you act unethically toward
the earth, it will return the favor—you'll cut yourself trying to pry a crystal or once you have it, it'll
drop out of your hand and seem to disappear."
Alex smiled. "If you don't have any questions, let's
go."

They didn't and by the time noon rolled around,
they had each filled a small bucket with quartz
and were all covered in red mud.

As Alex set down her bucket, she smiled at
Walker. "Glad we didn't take the Mercedes?"

"No kidding." Walker knocked a chunk of dried
mud off the side of his jeans. "You weren't joking
about filthy."

"I never joke about filth," Alex said with mock
seriousness. "Be warned, it's going to take a few
days for your hands to come clean. The red clay
leaves a faint pink-orange stain."

Walker looked at his palms, then over at Lacy,
who was still foraging through the pile of earth.
"Even if my hands were orange forever, it would
be worth it. She's having a ball."

"So you don't mind that she's getting filthy?"
she said, skeptically.

"Should I?"

"Not at all." Alex placed the loaded picnic basket

on the edge of the blanket she had spread over the soft earth. "It's just that some parents are . . . concerned with that type of thing."

"Oh?" Walker pulled his dark brows together in a frown. "What type of thing is that?"

Alex paused, then shrugged. "That their daughters look like little dolls."

"And you thought I was that kind of father?"

She met his eyes. "Was I wrong?"

Walker thought of Lacy's mother, of her obsession with physical beauty—and her criticism of a small, bruised baby. Anger raced through him so suddenly, it took his breath away. When he finally spoke, his voice was harsh. "Yes, you were wrong."

Alex lowered her eyes. Her comment had angered him. It was clear from the muscle that worked in his jaw, the rigid set of his shoulders, the pain in his eyes. "I'm sorry," she said quietly. "My own parents were of the opinion that girls should play with dolls and go to teas wearing white ruffles. They measured me, and themselves as parents, on how well I fit that stereotype. Unfortunately, I didn't fit at all."

"You weren't happy."

It wasn't a question but she replied anyway. "My mother used to say that when the Lord was passing out the sugar and spice and everything nice, I got an overdose of spice." Alex met his eyes. "I wanted to make them happy; I tried to fit their ideal of a perfect little girl." She laughed then. "But I would always blow it—come in with my dress muddied from digging in the garden, or with my hair tangled and knees skinned from climbing trees."

The picture she painted made him smile. It also

explained a lot about her, and about why she'd befriended Lacy. "How long did you keep trying?"

"To please them? Until I'd graduated from college and almost married their type of husband." She shuddered. "The type of man whose idea of a marriage was smiling civilly over coffee in the morning and sharing the financial section of the evening paper."

Even as he smiled, Walker acknowledged that boring wouldn't do for her. She had too much life, too much fire. She was a woman who would feel constrained by polite society, by doing what was expected, what was right. She was a woman who would have to bend what she believed to fit into a world like his.

As the truth of their differences struck him, his gaze skimmed over her. Neither her clothes nor posture were revealing or provocative, but there was something sensuous about her. It was more than the way her damp T-shirt clung lightly to her breasts or the way her jeans molded to her long, shapely legs. No, there was something sensual about *her*, something that had him thinking about sun and sweat and cool shadows. And sex. Hot, mindless, and breath stealing.

Walker shook his head, hoping to clear it, hopping reality would intrude. He silently swore when an image of red hair against white, white skin filled his head.

"And you almost married such a man?" he murmured finally, his voice thick.

Alex met his gaze, and her pulse scrambled. There was heat there, a fire ready to ignite, a bomb the moment before detonation. With the heat there was control—the kind that would stretch passions to the snapping point and make pleasure almost unbearable.

She dampened her suddenly parched lips. "Yes," she said, her voice barely more than a whisper. "I backed out a week before the wedding. My parents said I'd never find anyone else . . . as . . . suitable."

Walker touched her flushed cheek. It was satin and fire under his fingers. "His loss. Not yours."

Alex moved her head, just a little, so his fingers trailed across her cheek. Just as they reached the corner of her mouth, Lacy called out. It took no more than a second for them to react, yet to Alex it seemed an age because in that moment she felt regret and relief, shock and denial.

She took a step back; Walker dropped his hand. Both turned in the direction of the pit.

"Dad, Alex, I found a big one! Come see!"

Alex saw her chance to escape and took it. "You go, Walker. There's a small lake just to the left of here. I need to wash up before lunch."

"Fine." He shoved his hands into his pockets and backed away from her even more. "I'll go."

"Good." She fixed her gaze on the point over his left shoulder and prayed she didn't sound as rattled as she felt. "I'll unpack the picnic basket when I get back."

"Terrific." He swung around. "I'm sure Lacy is starved."

"I'm sure." Alex stuffed her hands into her pockets. "Okay then, well . . . bye." Without another word and assuring herself she was *not* running, she turned and headed for the lake.

*　　*　　*

It turned out that all Lacy had found was a rock, but she insisted there *was* a big crystal there waiting for her to discover it. She pleaded with Walker to let her dig just a little while longer before quitting for lunch. After making her promise not to wander from the pile and to call him if she started to feel sleepy, Walker acquiesced.

Alex wasn't back yet and Walker squinted up at the clear blue sky. She hadn't exaggerated about the heat or the lack of shade. He took off his hat and ran his fingers through his damp hair. Imagining dipping his hands in cool lake water, he started in the direction she'd headed only minutes before.

He found her, and the lake, a moment later. She was at the edge of the water. She'd undone her braid and was pulling her fingers slowly through the mass of fiery hair that tumbled around her shoulders. As he watched she squatted down and caught a bowlful of water with her cupped hands.

His breath lodged in his throat as she arched her neck and the water ran over her face and throat, soaking her shirt, plastering it to her. The water was icy, he could tell by her body's response . . . and his. Reminding himself who she was and why he was here, he headed toward her.

Alex looked up when he was almost upon her and smiled brightly. "Where's Lacy?"

"Still digging." It took all his control to keep his gaze trained on her face. "Her crystal turned out to be a garden-variety rock but she's determined to keep looking."

"I'm glad she's enjoying herself."

"She is." Walker slapped his hat against his thigh. "Alex, I feel I need to apologize."

"For what?" She was combing her fingers through her hair and water glistened on her lips and eyelashes. He had a wild urge to taste each drop with the tip of his tongue. Urges like that would get him in trouble, he knew, but recognizing the truth of that didn't help the ache. He told himself to look away, but didn't move a muscle. "I feel I . . . overreacted about this. About you."

She tipped her head back and smiled. "So, you think, maybe, I'm not so dangerous after all?"

He gazed down at her. Her eyes were laughing, her lips slightly parted and damp. The feelings he'd had minutes ago when he'd caressed her cheek, the ones he thought he'd controlled, if not conquered, raced over him. Her own hands were still tangled in her hair. Red hair against white, white skin. He took a step closer. "I wouldn't say that."

Alex saw his eyes, already dark, darken more. Her heart slammed against her ribs. "No?"

Walker moved a fraction closer. She made him feel reckless. She made him feel twenty again and fearless. She made him wonder how he'd lived so long without those feelings. "No," he murmured, reaching out and covering her hands, then moving them so he could tangle his own fingers in her hair.

The strands were like mink against his skin— silky soft and luxurious. He tightened his fingers, applying the softest, most subtle of force. Her head fell back; her neck arched; he pressed his lips to the flesh he'd made vulnerable.

Her skin was damp and salty; he was instantly addicted. It was smooth and hot—like heated brandy or warmed butter. He wondered what his life had been like before he'd tasted her. He found the pulse throbbing at the base of her throat and plundered it. When she made a sound of pleasure, of need, he sought the one behind her ear and did the same.

Alex curled her fingers around his shoulders. A moment before she had splashed cool water on her face and told herself she had put everything in perspective—he was an attractive man, she'd been alone for a long time, she was only drawn to him because he was wrong for her. She'd even convinced herself she could control her feelings. But a moment ago his lips hadn't been against her, her heart hadn't been thundering in her chest.

She arched her back even more; her breasts pressed against him. She found knowing he would feel her excitement in their hard tips erotic.

The blood rushed to her head as he murmured something low and only for her. A second later his mouth covered hers. His kiss didn't coax or woo, it demanded. And she responded, without pause or question. This man, with his conventional life and civilized ways, had surprised her. She had expected a soft, practiced kiss—she'd gotten rough and untamed. She had been confident she could control him, instead she had found herself to be persuasible. She parted her lips.

Walker caught her tongue with his own. He'd thought the taste of her skin addictive. Her lips were more so. He'd thought her initial response dizzying. Her response now defied description. She excited him in a way no other woman ever had.

"Alex, I want you."

His murmured words were urgent, demanding and she felt suddenly as if she couldn't breathe. With the sensation came reality . . . and truth. She wasn't afraid he would smother her; she was afraid she would let him.

She tightened her fingers for one more moment of madness. If only his touch weren't like magic against her skin, if only she didn't feel completely and utterly alive in his arms. Ironic that her body could feel so alive with a man who could, without design, kill her spirit.

She opened her eyes. His were already open, the passion in them undeniable. "You don't even know who I am," she said, not caring that the husky quality of her voice gave her away.

"I don't care." He lowered his hands and cupped her. "It doesn't matter."

"Yes." His arousal was evident and Alex sucked in a deep breath, needing the oxygen, letting it steady her. "It does. I'm wrong for you, Walker, and I refuse to be anyone but who I am. Not even for an afternoon."

"I'm not asking—"

"You would." She curled her fingers into the soft fabric of his shirt, gazing past him for a moment at the sparkling surface of the lake. She met his eyes once again. "You're the man who likes things that make sense, things that fit into neat packages. Remember?"

"I can make an exception."

"I don't think so." Relief washed over her. She realized she was in control again, she wouldn't waver. She was safe.

Alex smiled then, looking back at the water, an idea taking shape. She shouldn't do it, but it was so tempting. Too tempting. One little nudge and he would be in the lake. The water would be cool and clean and sweet—and he would be furious.

"Sorry, Walker"—Alex uncurled her fingers, relaxing her grip so they splayed against his chest—"but some things never will fit." With that, she pushed.

A second before she did, he read it in her eyes. He grabbed her arms just in time, they toppled together into the lake.

Alex came up sputtering. "Of all the dirty tricks."

Walker laughed and shook the water out of his dark, curly hair. "See, we're more alike than you think."

"In your dreams." She pushed at the wet hair hanging in her eyes. "I'd like to remind you, that you're the one who needed cooling off, not—"

"Hey! You guys didn't say you were going swimming. No fair!"

Both Alex and Walker turned their heads. Lacy and Heinz were at the top of the hill glaring down at them. As Walker started to pull himself out, Alex knocked him off balance and dunked him. "Come on in," she called, laughing and using her free hand to motion to the girl.

Lacy was hesitant at first, never having swum in an open body of water. With encouragement the girl inched into the water, then in no time at all was splashing and giggling. Each took a turn dunking the other two although Alex avoided meeting Walker's eyes. She also studiously avoided his touch and once when the side of her breast brushed against his arm she had to bite her lip to keep from flinching.

They played for some time until Lacy began complaining of hunger. Then the three of them dragged themselves up to the blanket only to find Heinz sprawled across the center of it.

"I'm surprised you're not fat," Alex scolded the dog. "You should have been down there with us exercising. Now up." He whined, his tail thumping against the ground.

"Come on, Heinz." Lacy sat at the edge of the blanket and patted the spot beside her. She didn't have to ask twice; the huge dog got up and ambled over to her.

Alex unpacked the basket, frowning as she noticed her fingers were still a little unsteady. Thirty minutes had passed since her encounter with Walker and she still felt as if her every nerve ending was on fire. She shook her head, willing away the sensation.

"Fresh-squeezed lemonade," she said, taking out a thermos and cups, hoping she'd injected just the right amount of brightness into her voice. "It's sweetened with honey." She poured them each a glass, then dug back into the basket, pulling out a plastic container and several foil-wrapped squares. "Homemade granola, and cucumber and sprout sandwiches."

"Cucumber and sprouts?" Lacy sounded disbelieving.

Walker lifted a slice of the bread to peer in at the contents, then looked back at her. "Maybe I shouldn't have eliminated tofu so quickly."

Alex placed her hands on her hips and shot them both a narrow-eyed glance. "They're delicious and healthy. Really, Walker, and you're a doctor."

Chastened, they both ate a sandwich and even Lacy admitted they tasted much better than they sounded.

"I don't want to stop looking," Lacy said after a while, grabbing a handful of granola. "I know there's a really great crystal in there just waiting for me."

Walker looked doubtfully at his daughter, then over at Alex. "How often do you find the large, perfect quartz crystals?"

"I never have. It's rare for individuals like ourselves to do so, the mining company gets the pick of what's there. But it does happen. I have a story—I swear it's true—about the very thing Lacy's feeling."

"A story? Like what I'm feeling?" Lacy munched on the crunchy snack. "What is it?"

Alex leaned back on her elbows. "One day I was up here digging. There was no one else around except for three elderly ladies. They asked me to stop humming because they couldn't hear the song of the crystals. Apparently, they had heard the song in Florida, packed up, and driven to Arkansas."

"Really?"

Walker made a skeptical noise. Alex sneaked a glance at him—he looked as doubtful as he sounded. "Here's the incredible part. I stopped humming and a few minutes later they each walked straight to a large, perfect crystal. Then they went home. I was astounded."

"Wow." Lacy reached for another handful of granola.

Walker snorted. "Is this some sort of crystal propaganda?"

"It's true." Alex held up her hands. "Every word."

"So what I'm feeling is the song of the crystal," Lacy said seriously.

"Could be." Alex looked at the child, knowing her next words would anger Walker. "Some people believe that crystals are here to give us ancient messages and to help us with our lives here on earth. They also say that specific crystals are meant for specific people and you can't own a crystal that's not for you. If this crystal belongs to you, you'll find it."

Lacy looked at her for a moment, her brow furrowed with thought. She stood then and brushed her hands on the side of her pants. "I'm going back to work. I know it's there waiting for me." She plopped her straw hat back on her head and looked at them both sternly. "You guys be quiet so I can hear the song."

The silence was heavy as Walker frowned at his daughter's retreating back. Alex lay back against the blanket, pretending nonchalance, knowing a confrontation was in the air.

When Walker was certain Lacy was out of earshot, he turned toward Alex. "We need to talk."

Alex tipped her hat over her face. "About what?"

"You promised you wouldn't mention anything about—"

"I did not," she interrupted, her voice muffled by the hat. "You asked me not to, I didn't agree."

"Dammit, that's semantics." He narrowed his eyes. "I thought we had a deal."

Alex lifted the hat and met his gaze. "What's wrong with an idea, Walker? Electricity, polio vaccinations and space flight all started out as ideas. Once upon a time people ridiculed Christopher Columbus for thinking the world was round; he proved them wrong. Brought before the Inquisition, Galileo was forced to renounce his ideas;

today we study them. Ideas can't hurt, they can only broaden."

"You make pretty speeches, Alex," he said in a dangerous tone. "But you're wrong. Ideas can hurt when you're talking about a vulnerable girl who desperately wants to believe in miracles."

Alex pulled herself into a sitting position and faced him. "You want to believe just as desperately."

It was true, he'd admitted that very thing to himself many times. But he understood that wishes and reality rarely met. He faced her just as squarely, just as confidently. "The difference is, I'm old enough to know there's no such thing. I'm old enough not to be crushed when a miracle doesn't come along and save the day."

"And one won't ever come for you because you won't open yourself to the possibility. You're all closed up, Walker. You've shut yourself off from life." She pushed her hair, dry now and wild, away from her face. "When did it happen? Why?"

"I've shut myself off?" He lifted his brows in disbelief. "What about you? You live all alone in the middle of nowhere and wear dimestore T-shirts that proclaim your philosophy on life." He swept his gaze over her. "What are you hiding from, Alex? What miracle are you waiting for but are too afraid to seek out?"

He hit so close to the mark she blanched. Furious, she angled her chin up. "I thought we were talking about Lacy."

"There's nothing more to discuss."

Alex curled her fingers into the rough texture of the blanket. "You may be her father but—"

"There's no 'but' there, Alex. I am her father. I decide what's right for her and what's not."

"—but that doesn't mean you're infallible. Or that you never make a mistake. Why won't you listen to what I have to say? How can you be so sure I'm wrong?"

"I don't have to be sure, as long as I have doubt. And I do." He stood. "You were right, Alex, we're too different even for an afternoon of fun. I'm going to inform Lacy that we're leaving."

Alex watched him walk away, her heart thumping against her chest. Something strange had happened while they argued—it had become personal. Making him believe what she thought had become more than an attempt to help Lacy, more than the want for a moral victory or even stubbornness. It had become a gut-wrenching want to reconcile their differences.

Why? Alex grabbed her hat and stood, then nervously tapped it against her thigh. Surely not to justify her desire to sleep with him? She rejected the thought even as it made her cheeks heat.

And it certainly wasn't because she was beginning to care for him. Alex gritted her teeth and shoved her hat onto her head. Because she wasn't.

Maybe her first answer had been the correct one after all, she told herself and started for the pit. It was only her hormones, only her body betraying her mind. Sure it was.

Halfway to the pit she noticed she no longer heard anything from Walker, Lacy, or even Heinz. She picked up her pace, then started to run, a funny sensation in the pit of her stomach. As she rounded the side of the pile of earth, she came to an abrupt halt. Walker was sitting next to Lacy, an arm around her shaking shoulders. Heinz was beside them, nudging the girl's arm with his nose. Alex's heart jumped to her throat. Something had happened to Lacy.

She squeezed her eyes shut, said a quick prayer, then opened them. "What's wrong?" she asked, her words choked, her chest tight.

But it was Lacy who looked up at her then, not Walker. The girl's eyes were wide. "I found it, Alex. I found my crystal."

Five

Hours later, Walker stood out on his patio, the cottage behind him in darkness, the wooded grounds before him darker still. Lacy slept inside, a peaceful, normal sleep born of sunshine and too much excitement.

The midnight air was cool and damp. Walker frowned as he lifted his coffee cup to his lips.

He wanted Alex. Hours had passed since he'd held her, and he still wanted her with a ferocity that left him shaking.

He set the cup down so sharply some of the hot beverage sloshed over the rim of the cup. Dammit, he shouldn't have given in to the temptation of kissing her. He shouldn't have allowed himself to wonder, even for a moment, how her mouth would taste.

But he had. Now he had to decide what to do about the craving that had been instant and that he knew wouldn't go away. He braced himself against the brick step wall that circled the patio and stared out at the black line that was the horizon. To see her and not touch her was out of the question. Even after only one kiss he knew the kind of control that would take, and he wasn't a masochist or into self-deprivation. Refusing to allow Lacy to see her or to let her go alone to visit Alex weren't even options. There was only one logical choice.

He and Alex would become lovers.

A thread of excitement curled through him at the thought, and he tipped his face up to the starstrewn sky. Oh, she would resist him . . . but not for long. She was a passionate woman—about her beliefs, her freedom. That passion carried over to other, less cerebral things—her response to him had been as fiery as her hair.

Walker closed his eyes and thought of soft, white skin, curves that were even more so and then, oddly, of the way her quartz crystal pendant nestled between her breasts. The crystal had radiated the heat of her body against his fingers, and he'd been aroused. He'd wanted to see her naked but for the gleam of silver and quartz against ivory flesh; he still did.

Walker opened his eyes and scowled. This afternoon it had been Lacy's crystal that disturbed him. They'd all been stunned when she'd found it, even Lacy. The trip back to Alex's had passed in a strange, almost pregnant silence. When they'd reached the cabin, Alex had explained the cleaning process, and Lacy had been upset to learn that the crystal would have to soak overnight in oxylic acid if she wanted to get the red oxide off. It had worried him that Lacy had been reluctant to give up her crystal even if only for the night.

There was a lump in his throat, and he swallowed past it. Lacy finding that crystal put him in an awkward position. How could he caution his daughter against believing in crazy notions about magic minerals, when the magic seemed to be happening? He knew finding the crystal had been luck. Mere coincidence. Not magic. Not some ancient message with her name on it . . .

Walker downed the last of his coffee. It was cold and bitter and he grimaced. He believed in logic. He had carefully mapped out his life, choosing to follow the conservative path of his parents. He had done everything in the correct fashion, working toward each new goal he set for himself until he'd achieved it.

Walker set aside the cup and slipped his hands into the pockets of his navy twill trousers. Then the marriage he'd thought as perfectly planned as everything else in his life had fallen apart, and from that point on it had seemed as if equilibrium had been just beyond his grasp.

Now he feared he was losing not only his control, but losing Lacy as well. He stuffed his hands deeper into his pockets. There, he'd admitted it. For all his goals and methodologies, he couldn't control Lacy's burgeoning independence or her obsession with Alexis Clare.

Or his own obsession with her.

Walker thought he heard a sound from inside and turned toward the darkened cottage. All was silent, but he went to the sliding glass doors to check anyway. Even though he still heard nothing, he slid the door open and headed for his daughter's room.

She was sleeping soundly, her favorite stuffed animal, an oversize pink rabbit, clutched against her chest. Her hair spread out over the pillow creating a dark fan, her eyelashes repeated the shape in miniature against her cheeks. She'd wiggled out from under her blankets, and Walker covered her again, then leaned down to place a light kiss on her cheek.

He'd never known it was possible to love like this. He couldn't have imagined love could be so terrifying. Nor had he ever been one to second-guess himself. Until Lacy.

He trailed a finger over her cotton-candy cheek; she smiled a little as she slept. Maybe he should end this vacation early. He could use the hospital as an excuse. He could promise Lacy another trip, one to someplace tropical, as soon as the invented crisis had passed.

Walker sighed. He couldn't do that. Lacy would be crushed. She adored Alex; she seemed to be flourishing under her attention.

He curled his fingers into fists, guilt eating at him. Lacy needed a woman's influence, she needed a mother. He should have looked for one long before this. After all, Victoria had walked out nearly four years ago.

Victoria. Just thinking of her left a bitter taste in his mouth, and he swallowed past it. He'd been incensed when she'd written a few months earlier, begging to see Lacy. He couldn't chance the what ifs, not with Lacy. His daughter couldn't stand another rejection.

She whimpered then and rolled from her side to her stomach; her rabbit dropped to the floor. Walker smiled as he bent to pick it up. Lacy had been disappointed so many times in her life, and been happy too few. He couldn't take her present enjoyment away from her, even if he felt it was in her best interest.

So they would stay. He and Alex would become lovers, and in so doing he would solve two of his problems—assuage an ache of desire such as he'd never felt before and regain a modicum of control.

After placing another kiss on his daughter's cheek, he turned and left the room.

Amazing. Alex stared at the crystal cupped in her hands, Lacy's crystal, and her fingers trembled, just a little. It was an incredible piece. She had only a few in the shop of this size and quality and they sold for several hundred dollars.

But she was shaken by more than the beauty and rarity of the piece—it was the circumstances of "the find" that unnerved her. Walker thought it luck, an inopportune coincidence. He didn't have to tell her, she knew.

But she didn't believe in luck, she didn't think there were coincidences. Everything in life rhymed, everything happened for a reason. Sometimes the rhyme or reason just wasn't apparent.

Like the sparks between her and Walker.

Alex frowned and placed the crystal in a drawstring bag made of the softest flannel. She wanted to deny the electricity that crackled whenever they were together but she was too honest. She wanted to call it a fluke, a mistake, but to do so would deny what she believed about life. So she was stuck. She and Walker were undeniably attracted to each other; it wasn't a mistake; it wouldn't go away.

Annoyed, she yanked on the strings of the bag. She didn't have to yield to the attraction. She hoped Walker was as eager to avoid her as she was him, because if he touched her she didn't think she would be able to resist temptation.

Heart hammering in her chest, Alex checked her watch, then started gathering together the things they would need to clean the rest of the crystals they found yesterday—old toothbrushes, a crock pot. Last night she had cleaned Lacy's "find," but today the three of them would clean the rest, and Walker and Lacy were due any moment.

No sooner had she collected the items than the bell over her shop's door tinkled. And as Walker stepped through it, she forgot her vows about distance and logic. He made her head spin, her mouth dry. For that first moment, as she allowed her eyes to race greedily over him, as she acknowledged feeling as if she'd drunk too much spiked punch, she realized she'd never felt this way before.

With a sinking stomach, she also realized she was in deep trouble. Because as their eyes met, she saw she wasn't going to get what she'd hoped for—in his dark gaze something sultry, something bold that challenged. He was not going to ignore or avoid the spark between them.

A prickle of awareness eased up her spine, and Alex steeled herself against it. He wasn't going to make it easy for her, but that didn't change a thing. Tossing Walker a defiant glance, she greeted Lacy.

The next couple of hours passed quickly. Alex showed Walker and Lacy how to clean the crystals, and while they did she handled the unexpectedly steady flow of customers.

At noon Walker suggested lunch and Lacy accepted for her before she had a chance to form an excuse. Alex gritted her teeth when Walker didn't even try to hide his amusement. He obviously enjoyed her discomfort.

They went to a place just outside the resort called Granny's Kitchen. Granny's served only traditional southern favorites like fried chicken, butter beans, and cornbread. No sooner had they all ordered their chicken and creamed potatoes, than Lacy realized she'd left her crystal at the shop. After extracting a promise that she would go directly there and back without dallying or talking to anyone and Alex's assurance that it was safe, Walker allowed her to run and get it.

As she watched the girl walk away, Alex shifted in her seat and cursed her luck. Now the only thing between her and Walker was eighteen inches of Formica; her only chance of diversion a glass of too-sweet iced tea.

"Alone at last," Walker murmured, grinning wickedly.

He was bold, confident to the point of cocky, and devilishly handsome. Annoyed, Alex tipped her chin up. She preferred her men with a little less brash. "Too soon you mean."

Walker only laughed and lifted his glass of iced tea. "Fried chicken, Alexis? I thought you were a health nut."

Alex narrowed her eyes, slightly. "I am. Granny's chicken is one of my weaknesses."

Walker laughed again; the sound was low and impossibly suggestive. "Interesting." He drew the word out as he leaned forward. "You must have other . . . weaknesses. What could they be?" He trailed a finger slowly across the back of her hand. "I'd guess moonlight through lace curtains"—he reached the juncture of her thumb and first finger and dipped his finger inside to tease the sensitive flesh—"or maybe the first pungent flowers of spring." He traced the shape of one nail, then the next. "Of course there's always bluesy music on hot, still nights or slow, deep kisses that steal not only your breath"—he paused—"but your sanity as well."

Her mouth was dry, her pulse fast. Her hand trembled slightly under his and she silently swore. As hard as she tried to steel herself against it, all she could think of were his lips, insistent on hers and his hands, hot, demanding and . . .

"How about it, Alex?" He laced his fingers with hers. "We could spend the whole day discovering weaknesses we didn't even know we had."

The blood rushed to her cheeks as she realized just how close to acquiescence she was. She reined in her runaway thoughts and snatched her hand away from his. "I see I'm not the only one who can make pretty speeches," she muttered, hearing the hint of desperation in her own voice and cursing again. It was time to take the offensive. "We need to talk about what happened yesterday," she said, more boldly than she felt.

Walker lifted his lips in a confident smile. "Speaking of . . . weaknesses."

Her cheeks, already hot, burned; Alex ignored the color as well as his words. "We both know it was a mistake—"

"It?"

"Yes." She cleared her throat. "Our embrace."

"Our embrace," he repeated, sitting back in his chair and folding his arms across his chest. "Is that what you call it?"

Alex felt the stirrings of temper. "Of course. What would you call it?"

He smiled and leaned toward her once again. "A nine-point-five on the Richter scale might suffice. If not that, I'd place it somewhere between dynamite and an A-bomb."

"Or how about the tornado that took Dorothy to Oz?" she inserted with a coolness belied by her thundering heart. With the same forced nonchalance, she arched an eyebrow. "Really, Walker, I didn't know you had such a gift of imagination. And you, such a good Bostonian."

"Not imagination, Alex, we both know that." He lowered his voice. "Should I refresh your memory?"

Her pulse scrambled as she thought of the ways he could do just that. She folded her arms across her chest. "Everything you described is destructive. Just as we would be together. No, Walker, what we both know is, we're wrong for each other and should keep as much distance between us as possible."

"What about this, Alex?" He trailed his finger over the curve of her flushed cheek, stopping when he reached the very corner of her mouth. Her lips trembled, just a little, and he smiled. "Can this be wrong?"

She jerked her head back even though it took every ounce of her self-control to do so. "Stop and think, Walker. Yesterday we were at each other's throats. You're only doing this to—"

"To what?" Walker dropped his gaze to her mouth, then lifted it to hers once again. "Excite you? Get you into my bed? You're right, I am."

Her breath caught. Places that were already steamy, became hotter still. She grabbed her iced tea. The glass was cold and wet, she held onto it like a lifeline. "Why, Walker? You don't even like me."

"I do like you," he said softly, surprising himself. "You're energetic and kindhearted. You're genuine and guileless." He tangled his fingers in the tips of her fiery hair; it was as soft as down against his skin. "No, I don't believe in a lot of the things you do, and I think your lifestyle is a little bizarre. But that doesn't mean I don't like you."

There was a funny sensation in the pit of her stomach. It was warm and tingly and made her ache with yearning. She drew a deep, steadying breath only to find her heart had lodged in her throat. Damn him, she thought furiously, it would be so much easier to resist him if he would be honest. But then, he no doubt knew that. She straightened her spine. "I think a man who would lie to a woman just to get her to sleep with him is despicable."

Walker was silent for a moment, then met her accusing gaze evenly. "You want to believe that because it makes it easier to deny what you're feeling. I'm the honest one here, not you."

Through his composure she saw the anger in his dark eyes. Alex gritted her teeth. He was quite an actor. "Why do I find that so hard to believe?"

"I don't know." Walker dropped his hand. "Why don't you tell me, Alexis. You seem to be the one with all the answers."

"Okay"—she lifted her chin—"if you're being so honest, so up front, why don't you tell me about Lacy's mother."

Walker went absolutely still for ten seconds.

Alex regretted her hastily spoken words. But she couldn't take them back.

Walker picked up his teaspoon and spun it through his fingers. The metal was smooth but hard in his hand, and it seemed somehow appropriate that at that moment he should feel the need to talk about his ex-wife for the first time in years. He met Alex's eyes—eyes as artless as his wife's had been coy. "I haven't talked about her in four years. Not since the day she walked out.

"In fact," he said, his voice tight. "I haven't said her name since that day either." He lifted his glass in a mocking salute. "Victoria Lancaster Stevenson.

"We met in New York at a charity ball," Walker continued. "I had just finished my last year of medical school; she was the most beautiful, vivacious woman I'd ever seen."

Walker fell silent then, allowing himself to remember and, oddly, making comparisons between his ex-wife and the woman sitting across from him now. Victoria had been decorative, like the trimming on a Christmas tree, colorful and sparkling, yes, but not nearly so alive as Alex. Alex had substance. She led with her heart; she had fire. Victoria had never had enough depth for heart or fire. If she had, she never would have treated Lacy the way she did.

"She, like I," he said finally, slowly, "was from an old, moneyed family. We had friends and experiences in common—it seemed too good to be true."

He laughed then, the sound was angry, brittle. "I pursued her for weeks. She let me. I sent flowers, expensive trinkets . . . love notes. Finally she agreed to go out with me. We were married sixty days later." He met Alex's eyes. "Sounds like the perfect, storybook romance, doesn't it? A beautiful woman, an ardent man, and a whirlwind courtship with all the right trappings."

Alex's throat was dry. She felt not only his anger and his pain, but his bitterness as well. But somehow she sensed the pain was not for himself. She held her breath as she felt the first stirrings of sensation inside her. In a moment, she knew, the phantoms would start moving through her, and she wouldn't be able to hide that something was wrong.

Alex dropped her hands to her lap and willed the phantoms away. She curled her fingers into fists until she felt the sting of her nails biting into her palms. She had to maintain a semblance of objectivity here, if not for her own sake, for Lacy's. She was certain this was the key to the youngster's illness. "What happened?" she asked, when she thought she had her voice, hoping Walker wouldn't notice the tremor.

He crumpled his paper napkin. "The perfect romance was nothing but a grade B movie. She found another man, one who was more exciting, one with a greater sense of adventure, and walked out. Lacy was six."

"She left Lacy?" Alex couldn't comprehend a woman leaving her child. She wasn't so naive as to think it didn't happen, and alarmingly often, but it still left her heartsick.

"No, she couldn't leave her," Walker said bitterly. "How could she, she was never with her." He picked up the teaspoon again, then set it back down. "A few days ago you asked why Lacy was so insecure, why she didn't even want to look into a mirror. Do you still want to know?"

Alex saw his fingers flex, saw the muscle that worked in his jaw, and she swallowed. She wasn't at all sure she wanted to know, but nodded anyway.

"To Victoria, beauty was everything . . . the problem was, Lacy was not a pretty baby. She was beat up from a breech delivery, twenty-one inches long, and only five pounds. She wasn't an easy baby either and had one childhood malady after another, starting with colic." He looked away. "The truth is, Victoria was repulsed by Lacy from the beginning. Worse, she didn't try to hide it. Maybe the marriage would have lasted if I'd felt the same way."

"But you didn't," Alex said softly, seeing what she'd had only glimpses of before, the whole man, the sensitive man beneath the rigid exterior.

"No." A smile touched his mouth. "I adored her. I still do." A moment later, the smile faded. "I did everything wrong. I thought I should try to keep the family together. I tried to placate Victoria and make up to Lacy for her mother's inexcusable behavior. I even thought it was working. What a fool."

"Oh, Walker. Don't—"

"I should have seen what she was doing to Lacy," he said, cutting Alex off. "I should have seen the harm she was causing. Instead of trying to keep the family together, I—"

"Don't," Alex said again, covering his hand with hers. " 'I should haves' will do nothing but make you sick. You did what you thought was right, you can't beat yourself up for that. You shower your daughter with love every day, that's a lot more than many kids get."

He moved his thumb against her palm. "It's not enough."

"No," she murmured, "sometimes it's not. But

there are times it's all we can do." Their eyes met and the silence stretched out between them. It wasn't uncomfortable, Alex thought, nor was it filled with the sexual tension of earlier. It was . . . companionable, the kind of silence that occurs between two people who have shared something of themselves and been accepted, understood.

The silence was broken by Lacy. She rushed up to the table, sliding into the booth next to her father, the flannel bag clutched in her right hand. "What were you guys talking about? You look so serious?"

Walker touched her hair as he met Alex's eyes. "Nothing, Muffin."

"I got it." She held up the bag, then looked around for the waitress. "Our food's not here yet? Gosh is this place slow."

Walker chuckled. "I asked them to hold our order until you got back. You wouldn't have wanted it to be cold, would you?"

Lacy released her breath in a long sigh. "I wouldn't care how it was, I'm starved!"

Lacy's whine was as uncharacteristic as it was thoroughly ten years old, and Walker and Alex laughed. From that point on the conversation was easygoing, the atmosphere light.

Even so, Alex couldn't shake the melancholy that seemed to have settled over her. So much sadness, so much pain. She twisted the napkin that lay over her lap. The truth was, her gift aside, she had grown to care for both these people. She cared about what happened to them—now, in the future, and in the past.

So much for protecting herself, she thought, looking up as the waitress came over with their food. She was more involved than she'd ever been—she'd set herself up for a big hurt when Lacy and Walker returned to Boston.

Because return they would, and she would be alone again. Alex frowned. She didn't mind being alone—she enjoyed it, she'd chosen this life.

Except that before, there hadn't been anybody to miss.

"Not hungry, Alex?"

She jerked her gaze from Lacy to Walker, then looked down at her plate. "Starved," she murmured, realizing she was.

The chicken was delicious, crispy on the outside and juicy on the inside, the creamed potatoes and gravy were deep south through and through. When they'd finished the meal and started back to the shop, Lacy brought up the three of them getting together again.

"Well," Alex hedged, feeling the need to protect herself, "you'll have to pick up your crystals. They'll be ready tomorrow."

"You can keep mine," Lacy said. "I have the one that's meant for me."

"But you can give them to your friends," Alex said. "I'm sure they'll be impressed when they learn you dug them yourself."

"I don't have many friends in Boston. And nobody nearly as nice as you." She slipped her hand into Alex's and looked up at her. "You can sell them in your shop."

The girl's words tugged at her heartstrings, and Alex squeezed her hand.

"Besides"—Lacy skipped along beside her—"that's not what I meant. When are we going to go someplace again?"

Alex made the mistake of looking down at Lacy's expectant and open face. She swallowed.

She couldn't disappoint the child, she just couldn't. "Next Sunday is the annual clean-up in Lake Catherine State Park. Volunteers pick up trash along the lake and in the park." She smiled. "They need all the volunteers they can get."

"You're going to spend the day picking up garbage?" Lacy's voice was incredulous.

Alex laughed and squeezed her hand again. "That about covers it."

"We'd like that, wouldn't we, Muffin?" Walker said, winking at Lacy. "But what about this Sunday?"

"This Sunday," Alex repeated.

"Your shop's closed isn't it?"

"Yes, but—"

"Yea!" Lacy clapped her hands. "I want to go to Magic Springs Fun Park!"

Alex sighed. Walker knew what a soft touch she was when it came to Lacy and had used it against her. The rat. She smiled at Lacy then shot him a withering glance. What could she do but acquiesce?

Six

The Sunday of the clean-up dawned clear, bright, and cool. It was the first hint of fall in a September that had been unseasonably warm. The leaves would have already started turning up north in the Ozark country, but here in the Ouachitas the dramatic shift from one color to a blaze of many came a little later, usually by mid-October.

Alex drew in a lungful of the crisp air and looked around her. Autumn was worth waiting for. Already hints of reds and golds dotted the forest, soon yellows, oranges, and even deep purple would be the rule rather than the exception.

Alex slid a glance at Walker. A frown pulled at his mouth and wrinkled his brow. He obviously wasn't enjoying the great outdoors.

She followed his gaze, knowing where it would lead—Lacy. She'd fixed the girl up with a couple of the kids she knew from around the resort, and right now they were laughing as they waited in line for trash bags.

She glanced back at Walker, a fluttering sensation in the pit of her stomach. He was wearing an off-white fisherman's cable-knit sweater and soft blue denims. The sweater was thick, bulky, and heart-stoppingly masculine: the jeans were form fitting and distracting as hell.

She was in deep trouble.

She slipped her hands into her pockets as the urge to lay her hand over his arm raced over her. The last week and a half had been fun. They'd gone sightseeing and although she'd seen all the sights before, she'd enjoyed playing tourist again. Fitting in the shop and their many excursions had been wild, but in the end they'd seen all the attractions Lacy had wanted to and several that she hadn't.

Alex dug her hands further into her pockets. And through it all, Walker had kept up the seduction he had started that day at lunch. He'd cajoled and complimented and charmed; he'd used every opportunity to touch her, to whisper into her ear, or send her long, smoldering looks.

A tingle eased up her spine, and Alex scowled. Against her will, against her better judgment, his seduction was working. She couldn't sleep, eat, or work for thinking of him—of being in his arms, his mouth on hers, his hands fevered and urgent against her skin.

Her scowl deepened as she shot him a surreptitious but withering glance. She would never have guessed Walker to be a tease but in the past days he'd proven otherwise. All that looking and touching hadn't led to anything more than a cold shower. Dammit, he hadn't even kissed her. Not once. She wasn't a woman given to petulance or pouting, but right now she felt like sticking out her lower lip and stamping her foot.

Alex narrowed her eyes remembering. Two days earlier Walker had had a tennis match, so she'd offered to take Lacy to the resort's outdoor mineral bath. It was the first outdoor bath, hot tub really, to be given the Department of the Interior's approval to use Hot Springs's celebrated thermal water.

"This feels great," Lacy had said, giggling and sliding further into the hot, bubbling bath. The tub was built into the side of the mountain and steam billowed off it into the cool evening air. "Too bad Dad can't be here."

"Mmm, too bad," she had murmured, not sorry at all as she'd relaxed against the side of the tub.

"Who says I can't be here?"

Her eyes had flown open at Walker's voice. As she'd looked up at him, her heart had sunk. Instead of his tennis whites, he was wearing one of those itsy-bitsy racing suits. And he had the body of a god. Her own body responded crazily, and she slid a little deeper into the bubbling tub. "What are you doing here?" she had asked, not caring that she sounded peevish.

"I cancelled my tennis game," he murmured, climbing in. "After all, how often do I get a chance to soak in the water that made Hot Springs famous?"

"And you can play tennis anytime," Lacy chimed in.

"Right, Muffin."

To Alex's dismay, he sat next to her. *Right* next to her, close enough so her every nerve ending screamed with awareness. But he didn't touch her, not quite, and she gritted her teeth. He knew exactly what he was doing. Well, she wasn't about to let him get to her!

Determined to relax, she'd once again leaned her head back and closed her eyes. It didn't work. Even in one-hundred-degree bubbling water every one of her muscles was tensed. She breathed deeply, in and out, concentrating on the oxygen as it filled her lungs and the soothing gurgle of the water. In a few minutes her muscles began to loosen and relax.

Alex lifted her lips in a small smile. After all, what could happen with Lacy in the tub?

"I'll be right back, you guys, I have to . . . you know."

This time when she snapped her eyes open, it was to see Lacy clear the tub and start toward the changing room. She shifted her gaze from the girl to Walker. He smiled lazily, and she was reminded of a cat surveying a cornered mouse.

"Well, well," he murmured. "Isn't this an interesting turn of events."

"Can it, Walker. Just stay on your side of the hot tub." She inched away.

He followed. "What are you afraid of, Alex? What I might do or your own response to me?"

"Neither." She tried to sound casual. "I told you the other day I wasn't interested in getting involved, yet you seem determined to prove something."

"I don't know what you mean." His expression was anything but innocent as he slid closer. "Have I kissed you?"

"No."

"Have I openly propositioned you?" He moved a fraction more in her direction. "In any way?"

Alex caught her bottom lip between her teeth. "Well . . . no . . ."

"Then what?" He tenderly brushed a lock of hair away from her face.

"That!" she exclaimed.

"What?" He gazed into her eyes.

Her pulse scrambled at his look, filled with hot, heady promises. She steeled herself against both his gaze and the sensations it produced. "The way you're looking at me, the way you're always accidentally touching me, the way—"

"Is it unpleasant?"

"No, but"—his thigh brushed against hers and her breath caught—"I want you to stop."

"Okay, Alex"—He reached and pulled her against his chest—"no more accidental touches."

His flesh was warm and strong against hers, she felt the tickle of crisp hair against the smooth curve of her breast. Nothing separated them except the thin fabric of her maillot, and she could feel the steady thump of his heart. She wondered if he could feel the runaway pace of her own.

"There's nothing accidental about this." He ran his hands over her shoulders and down to the small of her back. "Or this," he murmured, moving his fingers in small, mesmerizing circles.

Alex made a small sound of pleasure as he moved his hands again. This time they dipped lower, stroking places he had no right to, places she didn't have the strength to refuse him. She sagged against him. "Stop it," she whispered. The sound was breathy, feminine, and anything but a plea to stop.

"Stop what?" Walker asked, moving his fingers again. "This?" He lowered his head until their mouths were only a breath away. "Or this?"

"Yes." Alex curled her hands around his shoulders, but instead of pushing him away, she pulled him closer. "Yes, stop." Walker caught her bottom lip in a gentle nip. Her already elevated blood pressure skyrocketed.

"Okay," he'd murmured then, a smile tugging at his mouth. He'd dropped his hands and slid away. No cajoling or arguing or gentle pleas. She'd been left feeling more than a little ridiculous because the truth was, she hadn't wanted him to stop at all . . .

Alex sighed again.

"You sound like I feel."

Alex jerked her gaze to Walker's, surprised out of her reverie. "What?"

"You sighed."

"I did? Oh." Alex shoved her hands into the pockets of her corduroy slacks, then feeling pink stain her cheeks, pulled them back out. She didn't have to worry that he'd ask what she'd been thinking, his eyes had already drifted back to Lacy. She gave into the urge she'd resisted minutes ago and laid a hand on his arm. "She's going to be okay."

"I'm not so sure," he murmured, not looking at Alex.

"She needs some freedom, Walker." Alex shook her head. "After all, you can't watch her every second."

"I'm not going to take my eyes off her."

Alex rolled her own eyes, then turned as someone called her name.

"Alex, glad you could make it again this year."

"Russell! Hi." Alex smiled and shook hands with the boyish-looking park ranger. "I brought you a couple more volunteers." She introduced Walker, then pointed out Lacy.

"Glad to have you." He took off his hat and ran

a hand through his sandy hair. "The turnout's a little disappointing this year."

"I see that," Alex said. Last year's tally had been right at two hundred volunteers, this year it looked as if they would be lucky to have eighty. "Well, we're here and ready to work. Where would you like us to start?"

The man turned toward Walker. "The Girl Scout troop is taking the pontoon boat, I could hook your daughter up with—"

"No," Walker interrupted, "Lacy will stay with me. Thanks."

The ranger ran a hand through his hair again, then slid his cap back on. "It's just the three of you?"

"Five," Alex corrected. "Two of her friends are coming with us."

"Okay then." He turned and pointed toward the shore. "There are several small, flat-bottomed boats, Pete will assign—"

"No boats," Walker said sharply. "I'm sorry, but not with Lacy. Excuse me, I'm going to see how she's doing."

Confused and a little embarrassed, the ranger looked at Alex. "We provide life jackets if that's what he's worried about."

"It isn't," Alex said softly, watching as Walker put his arm protectively around his daughter. Poor Walker. She should have anticipated this. At their first meeting Lacy had told her that she wasn't allowed near the water and most of today's clean-up would be done by boat along the shoreline. She turned back to the ranger and smiled. "We'll take the nature trails, Russell."

He shrugged. "If you want. You know the procedure—there's no way to clean the whole park, so stick to the trails and turn back when the forest starts to get dense. The party will start at three, there're free drinks and other refreshments available until then."

"You got it." She saluted teasingly, then swung around and headed toward the girls and Walker. Thirty minutes later they were finishing up their first trail, walking behind the three girls. Walker had insisted they all stick to the same trail. The girls forged ahead, eagerly gathering every scrap they saw; consequently their own bags were almost empty.

"You want to talk about it?" Alex asked when she was sure the girls were out of earshot.

Walker angled her a questioning glance. "About what?"

"Your fear of Lacy drowning."

Surprised, Walker stopped and turned fully toward her. He stared at her for a long moment before speaking. "Is it so obvious?"

"Yes."

Walker shifted his gaze to a point over her left shoulder before meeting hers again. "A cousin of mine drowned. I was twelve when it happened and with a boy's imagination for the gross and terrifying, I obsessed on what it must have been like for him."

"You must have been very frightened."

He shrugged and slipped his hands into his pockets. "He was older and we weren't close, but I listened to the whispering of the adults and let my imagination run wild. The situation surrounding his death has nothing in common with Lacy's—he wasn't a narcoleptic; he'd been drinking—but my fear of something happening to her manifests most vividly in a fear of her drowning."

"That's understandable."

"Is it? I don't have objectivity anymore." Walker pulled his hands out of his pockets, then feeling restless, shoved them back in. "I know Lacy can't stay in her room for the rest of her life. I also know she wouldn't be happy if she did. But I can't help being afraid every time she walks out the door."

Alex nodded. "I empathize with how you feel, Walker. But I also know that Lacy needs air." She motioned to the three girls. They were all about the same age, but Lacy was markedly more naive, childlike. And although she was enjoying herself, she was also a little insecure. It was there in the tentative way she laughed, in the way she hung back slightly, from the other two. "She needs to be around kids her own age. She needs to feel like she's not so different."

Walker turned to her, a frown forming between his brows. Why couldn't Alex be what she appeared? A freethinking woman with a big heart and some kooky ideas? Why did she have to have moments when she made such good sense? "How did you get to be so smart?"

She grinned and started moving again. "Staying away from red meat is my guess."

Walker returned her smile. "I'm a doctor and I know there's no correlation between red meat and brains."

Alex sniffed and flipped her hair over her shoulder. "Well, my father's a doctor so I know there're a lot of things doctors don't know."

She was teasing, but it was his experience that what most people teased about was based on truth. She didn't particularly like doctors, she certainly didn't respect the profession. Walker glanced at her. The fact that her father was a doctor explained a lot; she'd already told him that she and her family didn't get along. He bent and picked up a piece of trash the girls had missed. He didn't know why her father being a doctor made him feel odd, but it did.

Suddenly he wanted to change her opinion, wanted to prove to her that she could care for him despite his profession. The girls had disappeared around a bend and without questioning his action, Walker stopped and pulled Alex into his arms. "Would you like to expound on that?"

"On what?"

"On the theory about what doctors do and don't know."

Alex splayed her fingers against his chest, his heart beat a steady rhythm beneath her palm. She resisted the urge to curl her fingers into the fabric of his sweater, tipping her face up to his instead. "We don't have that much time."

He moved his hands from her shoulders to the small of her back. "I'm not watching a clock."

Her pulse fluttered, despite her best intentions. "Well, I am and—"

"That's a shame," he said, moving his fingers in soft, slow circles. "Because there's something about the great outdoors that appeals to my sense of lust."

Her heart thundered against her chest. For a moment she thought she wouldn't be able to breathe around it. "Is that so?"

"Mmm-hmm." He trailed his hands back up to her shoulders, then cupped her face. "I don't know what it is." He ran his thumbs over her flawless cheeks. "Maybe it's the fresh air or the vast, untamed landscape, but whatever, it definitely makes me think about making love." He lowered his gaze to her mouth.

This was it, she thought, a small shudder moving through her. *Finally.* Alex slid her hands up to his shoulders and tipped her face up to meet his.

A long, breathless moment passed, then Walker dropped his hands. "I just wanted you to know that."

Alex stood stock still for twenty seconds, watching him walk away, her hands still lifted. Then, cheeks burning, she took off after him. Seconds later she had his arm and had swung him around. "Why are you doing this?"

Walker bit back a smile and met her gaze with what he hoped was cool disinterest. "Doing what?"

She pushed the hair away from her face impatiently. "Driving me crazy."

He arched a brow in question. "Define crazy."

She wanted to scream, she wanted to slap him. She wanted to kiss him more. Letting her breath out in a furious huff, she stood on tiptoe, reached up, and jerked his head down to hers.

She caught his laugh with her lips. It registered that he was laughing at her, probably because he'd gotten exactly what he'd wanted. She filed that away for later. She'd waited too long to again feel the touch of his mouth on hers to worry about who had the upper hand or how she'd been manipulated.

And his mouth felt wonderful—warm and firm and responsive. She wondered how she had held out so long. Her own laugh bubbled to the surface; she should have done this the first time he'd teased her. Maybe then she wouldn't have lost so much sleep.

Alex combed her fingers through his dark hair,

delighting in the tickle of his curls against them. He smelled manly, a delicious combination of sunshine and sweat. She parted her lips and caught his tongue—after all, if she was going to be the aggressor here, there was no room for shyness.

She didn't have to be the aggressor for long. With a groan Walker wrapped his arms around her and deepened the kiss. She tasted sultry and wild. She made him crazy. He dragged his mouth from hers to find the curve of her jaw, the arch of an eyebrow, the pulse throbbing behind her ear. All the while he acknowledged the truth.

She'd come to him, yes, but he had no control. He'd been mad to think he would be able to keep his head once she touched him.

She made a sound of pleasure and curled her fingers into his sweater. In that moment Walker realized that something had changed, that he'd changed. He wasn't sure why or even what was different, he only knew he felt like a caterpillar who had suddenly burst into the flight of the butterfly.

Uncomfortable with the sensation, Walker wrenched his mouth from hers. They were both breathing heavily; he fought to even his. This was about desire, he told himself. This was about the chemistry between two people. Nothing more. Even as he tried to convince himself, he stared down into her glazed eyes, darkened to emerald with passion, and need hit him in the chest with the force of a sledgehammer. She was hiding nothing, denying nothing. She wanted him, she would give him everything.

At that moment, for the first time, he wanted the everything her eyes promised—the passion, the laughter, the tenderness. And he wanted it with this woman. He caught her lips again.

They jumped apart at the sound of giggling.

"Our bags are full," Lacy said, her sparkling eyes going from Alex to her father and back.

Heart pounding, Alex shot Walker a glance as he cleared his throat. He looked as uncomfortable, as flushed, as she felt. She fought back a laugh: He didn't have the upper hand after all. Lacy did. Giving in to her need to, she laughed. A moment later they all were, even Walker.

The rest of the day passed quickly and happily. By the end of the day they'd filled thirty-two trash bags and were pretty proud of it. At the party they feasted on grilled hamburgers, baked beans, and potato chips. Even Alex ate some chips although no amount of ribbing could convince her to eat meat with her bun, instead she garnished the bread with tomato, lettuce, and mayonnaise. As the perfect ending to the day, Lacy's name was drawn for one of the grand prizes, a brightly colored wristwatch.

But the real ending of the day came much later and was much less perfect.

When they got back to Walker and Lacy's cottage, there was a woman waiting for them—Victoria Lancaster Stevenson-Ridgeman, Lacy's mother.

"What are you doing here?" Walker asked, snapping the door shut behind him. Alex winced at his tone and the way he closed the door. She said a silent prayer of thanks that Walker had allowed Lacy to go to the arcade with her two new friends.

"The manager let me in." Victoria swept her chestnut-colored hair, hair the exact color of Lacy's, away from her face with a dramatic flourish. "I told them I was your wife."

As Alex attempted to leave, Walker put a hand

on her arm. She paused, wanting to run but knowing he needed her with him. She felt his anger and his pain—it didn't take her gift to read his feelings, he shook with them.

"*Was* being the operative word," he said, his voice low, dangerous. "You have ten seconds to tell me what you want."

She arched one perfectly manicured eyebrow. "Where's Lacy?"

"You gave up the right to know that four years ago."

The woman's jaw tightened almost impercepti- bly. "I'm her mother."

"Again, a right you willingly gave up."

She paused as if reassessing her strategy, then changed it. "Please, Walker . . ." She stood and crossed to him, meeting his eyes beseechingly. "I want to see her. If you'd answered my letter, I wouldn't have had to force the issue like this. I really want to see her," she repeated.

"I don't care what you want, Victoria." His voice was cold and hard as steel, and it hurt Alex to hear him that way. "Please leave."

His ex-wife reached out to touch him, then as if thinking better of it, dropped her hand. "Please, Walker. I've come to realize what's important in life. I know now what I threw away. I need to see her, talk to her. Won't you let me try to make amends?"

Alex held her breath, hoping Walker would relent, hoping he would feel just a small tug of sympathy for this woman who was so obviously lost and aching. But instead she felt his muscles tense even more under her hand, saw the tighten- ing of his jaw.

"What happened to your artist? Did life get too

demanding for you? Did you pull another disappearing act? There's got to be some other reason for your being here than motherly love."

"He left me," she said quietly, lowering her eyes and wringing her hands. When she lifted them again they were filled with tears. Alex wondered if they were real or affected but was certain the woman was being honest even if her tears weren't. "He was irresponsible, grasping. I finally realized he didn't care about me at all—just about my money."

"I didn't mean to hurt her, Walker. I admit I was childish and selfish, but I . . ." Her voice trailed off. "I'd hoped it wasn't too late. I want to try, really try this time, to be close to her." She met his eyes. Alex's heart wrenched at the pain she saw there. "My life is empty, Walker. There's nothing there."

Walker drew in a sharp breath, wheeled around to face the sliding glass doors and the lovely landscape beyond. A moment later he turned back toward the two women. Alex cringed at the expression in his eyes—hatred for this woman burned inside him.

"You haven't changed, Victoria. Listen to yourself, you want to see Lacy for *you*, not for her. *Your* life is empty, *you* want back what you threw away. What about what's best for Lacy? What happens when you get bored and check out again? It is too late, Victoria. I won't allow you to hurt her and all your good intentions don't mean anything—because I know what you are."

Victoria drew back and slapped his face. When she tried it again, he caught her hand. His face was icy with rage. "Hell will freeze over before I'll let you near Lacy. If I have to I'll hire a guard to watch her twenty-four hours a day. Now get out before I throw you out."

Alex knew how hard that must have been for her to admit, but Walker was unimpressed. He dragged a hand through his hair. "Boy does this sound familiar."

She held out a hand again and this time she touched him. "I loved you, Walker. I did."

"Who are you trying to convince? Me or you?" He shook off her hand as if it were a rattlesnake. "When you love someone you don't do everything you can to destroy them. You don't take cheap shots, you don't walk out. Oh that's right, you said you loved me, not Lacy. You never loved her . . . did you?"

"I regret my past actions . . . I do. I know now what it feels like to—"

"To hold your child and try to comfort her after her mother ridicules her for the hundredth time? To rock your baby to sleep after she cried for hours for a woman who thought so little of her she didn't even say good-bye?" He curled his hands into fists. "No, you don't know what it's like and excuse me if I don't feel any pity that you got a taste, even such a small one, of your own medicine. When you walked out on Lacy, you destroyed any illusions she had of a loving mother and what was left of her own self-esteem. Now you're back for more. There's nothing left, Victoria."

The woman blanched, and this time Alex didn't wonder if her tears were real. There was a knot of tears in her own stomach—not for the woman or even the child, but for the man who couldn't forget or forgive.

Seven

Victoria Ridgeman left the cottage in tears. Alex watched her go, her own emotions reeling. She felt sorry for the woman, but she ached for Walker. As the door closed behind her, Alex turned to him. His face looked as if it had been carved from granite. His expression told her nothing of how he felt except for his eyes—they were naked with pain.

Her heart constricted. Walker valued control, admired restraint. He would hate it if he knew how much he revealed to her. As if he read her mind, he swung away from her and faced the windows once again.

His shoulders and back were rigid with his attempt to regain control of his emotions, and Alex fought the urge to go to him, to try to comfort him. Already his pain roiled inside her, to touch him would hurt too much. She drew a deep breath, let it out shakily, then drew another. The oxygen didn't help and the ache in her chest became almost debilitating.

She had to get out of here, Alex thought, a thread of panic winding through her. She'd only reached "overload" once before and it had been terrifying. She had thought, really thought, that she was going to die.

Alex took a step backward, then stopped. As fearful as she was, she couldn't bear to leave him alone.

He settled her quandary for her. "Alex . . . do me a favor?" His voice was choked, tight.

"Yes."

"Go find Lacy at the arcade. Stay with her . . . don't let her come back here for at least an hour." Looking over his shoulder, he met her eyes. "I don't want her to see me this way."

Relief washed over her, and she felt like the coward she was. "All right," she murmured, moving backward until her hand found the doorknob and closed over it.

"Alex?"

She twisted the knob but turned back to him. He hadn't taken his gaze from the window. "Yes?"

"I'm sorry I got you involved in this . . . mess."

It scared her to realize just how involved she'd already been. "Don't worry about it."

He continued as if he hadn't heard her. "I know how I must look to you." He drew a deep breath which sounded heavy, almost labored. "She seemed so heartbroken, so sincere—" He did meet her gaze then—"but she did things you couldn't imagine . . . subtle cruelties, the kind that break the spirit without bruising the flesh."

She longed to put her arms around him but couldn't move a muscle. "People can change," she said finally, thinking of Victoria, but more, of him.

He turned away from her once again. "I can't chance it, Alex."

You can't not, she thought, staring at his rigid back. There was so much she wanted to say to him, but now was not the time—for either of them. Instead, she reassured him in the only way she could. "You're a good father, Walker. I hope you know that."

She pulled the door lightly shut behind her. Resting her back against the cold wood, she squeezed her eyes shut and willed the phantoms away. Long moments passed. When she finally felt she could move without staggering, she started for the arcade, taking the path Lacy would be most likely to, not wanting to chance missing her.

Alex shivered as the wind cut through her sweater. She'd forgotten her gloves at the cottage so she rubbed her hands together as she walked. Even now, after the empathetic pains had disappeared, she was shaken, felt bruised and disheartened. She almost laughed out loud—disheartened? What a rational word that was to explain how she felt about what she'd witnessed between Walker and his ex-wife—and what she'd learned about Walker as a result.

Leaves crackled beneath her feet. She lowered her head. It wasn't that she blamed Walker for his anger—Victoria had done a number on both him and Lacy—she would be angry too. It was the depth of his anger, his hatred, that disturbed her. It ate at him, devouring those parts of him that had the capacity for love and forgiveness.

Without them, he could never love another woman.

Alex caught her bottom lip between her teeth.

That shouldn't matter so much, but it did. It seemed to matter more than anything. She had begun to care for him. She lifted her lips in an uncharacteristically sarcastic smile. There was another of those benign words—care.

She looked up at the gray, wintery sky. Wasn't the truth a lot stronger than that? Wasn't the truth that she had started to believe she could love him? And he her?

Yes.

Alex shivered again and crossed her arms across her chest to keep away the cold. Now she knew better. The scene she'd witnessed had swept away the last bit of her illusions. Or was delusion a better word to describe what she'd been doing to herself?

The arcade was in sight now and Alex thrust her hands into her pockets and tried to look cheerful. Now she had to think of Lacy; later when she was alone, she could brood about Walker and her own feelings.

Alex paused outside the arcade's swinging doors, a frown wrinkling her brow. She wasn't certain that keeping Victoria's visit a secret was the right choice, the girl had a right to know. But Walker would tell her, Alex assured herself. He was waiting for a better time, a time when he had a firmer grip on his emotions.

Alex frowned. Did she really believe that? That day over lunch, the day he'd talked about his life with Victoria, he'd told her he hadn't said her name in nearly four years. She'd gotten the impression he hadn't spoken of her either, that the subject was taboo. But if that was the case, who had Lacy gone to when she'd needed to talk about her fears and feelings of betrayal?

Nobody. The truth of that was staggering, and Alex caught her breath. Poor Lacy. How alone and scared she must sometimes feel.

From inside, Alex heard Lacy's now-familiar giggle and a rush of tenderness washed over her. It was time to stop tiptoeing around Walker and start helping Lacy. If her first notion had been to save herself and run, her second was to stay and try to heal Lacy despite the probable consequences.

She narrowed her eyes. She could help Lacy—she knew she could. And she would keep an emotional distance from Walker. That was a necessity. If nothing else, witnessing the scene between him and his ex-wife would fire her resolve.

Taking a deep breath, she pushed through the swinging doors and stepped into the arcade. The three girls looked up. "Okay, you sidewinders," she drawled in her best imitation of John Wayne, "step aside. I've got a score to settle with the baddest gunslinger this side of the Mississippi."

The next few days proved tougher for her than she could have imagined. Because although she knew with her rational self that a relationship with Walker would be impossible, her irrational self—her heart and hormones—weren't communicating. Each time she saw him the sexual pull she felt between them increased instead of the opposite. She found herself reaching out to touch him, found herself gazing at him, an ache of hunger inside her so strong it made her weak.

Of course, she did all these things when he wasn't looking—which was most of the time. It appeared that just as she'd been changed that afternoon, so had he. He was quieter, more reserved. He looked at her less, touched her almost not at all. He even allowed Lacy to see her without him being present—which would have warmed her if she thought he'd begun to trust her—but she suspected it had more to do with . . . she wasn't sure what.

Lacy also began to spend more time with Tracy and Tina, the girls she'd fixed her up with from the resort. One day while she and Lacy were playing shuffleboard, or rather, playing around at the shuffleboard, the two girls came up and asked Lacy if she would like to rent a minibike and go with them on a nature ride.

Alex took one look at Lacy's eager face and gave her permission even though she suspected there might be hell to pay when Walker found out. She was right.

Less than an hour later, Alex looked up from the stones she was arranging as the bell above the shop's door jangled. It was Walker. The collar of his jacket was turned up against the cold, his hair was mussed as if he'd run his hands through it. He smiled at her and her heart flip-flopped.

"Hi," she said with forced calm, going back to the crystals, hoping he wouldn't notice how her hands shook. She didn't question that what she'd done was right, but she knew Walker would be furious.

"Hi." He stepped into the store, looking around him. "Where's Lacy? In back?"

"No." Alex's fingers closed over a rose quartz, and she drew a deep breath. "She's with Tracy and Tina."

"Oh?" Walker drew his eyebrows together, immediately concerned. "Did they go to the arcade?"

Alex released the quartz and straightening, met his gaze. "They rented minibikes and went on a nature ride along Bear Pass."

For a split second Walker thought he'd misunderstood her. He saw by her expression that he hadn't. The panic started in the pit of his stomach and spread upward until he couldn't catch his breath. "How . . . long . . . ago did they leave?"

"It's okay, Walker," Alex said quietly. "She's fine. The paths they'll take are often used and quite safe. There's no water, no cliffs, or deep gull—"

"How long?"

His tone was low and dangerous, his expression more so. In that moment this civilized Boston doctor reminded her of Gunslinger Sam. She fought the urge to take a step back. Instead she lifted her chin and stood her ground. "About forty minutes."

"Dammit!"

As he turned toward the door she raced for it, blocking his way. "Walker, she'll be fine. She needs some independence, she needs some room to grow up."

He glared at her. "I can't believe you let her go."

Alex squared her jaw, knowing what the consequences of her words would be. "I encouraged her."

Walker flexed his fingers in fury and frustration. If he wasn't so civilized, he would happily strangle her. "Out of my way, Alex. I'm going after her."

"It's futile, Walker." She lifted her hands, palms up. "The path is accessible only by foot or bike;

by the time you rented a bike, she'd be on her way home."

He fought for control. "My God, Alex . . . a motorized vehicle! Anything could happen. What if she . . . I shouldn't have trusted you. I shouldn't have let down my guard, even for a moment."

She grabbed his arm, it was like steel under her fingers. "I talked to her first. I told her if she felt sleepy, to tell her friends and stop. She promised me she would." Alex gripped his arm tighter. "She lives with the disease, Walker, she knows what to do."

"Lord, Alex! What if she doesn't? What if—"

"You can't 'what if' for the rest of your life, Walker. Or hers. She has to be allowed some freedom, some friends. What are you going to do when she's a teenager? When she has her first date, when she goes away to college?"

He shook off her hand. "I'll deal with that when the time comes."

Alex grabbed his other arm. "Will you? Or by then will she be so frightened about what could happen, so insecure in herself and her abilities that her first date never comes, that she chooses not to go away to school or worse, not to chance it at all. After all, what if she fell asleep during a big exam? Or during a lecture? The bell could ring and everyone would file out, leaving her—"

"Stop it!" He grabbed her arms. It ripped him apart to picture what Alex was describing. It wasn't the life he wanted for Lacy. "I love my daughter. I have to protect her, she has no one else."

"Or is it that you have no one else?"

"Damn you, Alex."

His muttered curse was her only warning; a moment later his mouth came crashing down on hers. Alex would have stumbled backward under the force of his kiss had she not been holding his arms already. Without questioning her own actions, she curled her fingers into the fabric of his coat and pulled him closer.

She felt his fury, could taste it in his kiss. But more than anger fueled him—there was desperation in the way his hands caught at her hair, the way his hips challenged hers. She recognized the desperation because it mirrored her own.

Walker parted her lips and caught her tongue. He was unsure if he was trying to silence her because of what she said or because she was right. He only knew that the last few days, days of not touching her, had been hell. He wanted her in a way, with a passion, he'd never thought possible. His need was as numbing as it was exhilarating, his hunger dangerous in its single-mindedness.

Even knowing that, he deepened the kiss. Her mouth was ready for him, parted and eager, but he felt the resistance of her body. As, he knew, she must feel his. She didn't want this—and did—just as much as he.

He didn't give a damn. Not about who he was or she was, about their differences or even their similarities. This had nothing to do with thinking. He had to have her in his arms or die.

Not breaking the kiss, he bent her over his arm. She curled a leg possessively around one of his— an invitation for an embrace of another sort.

He tore his mouth from hers. They stared at each other for long moments, their breath coming in small gasps, their hands clutching at each other, both refusing to acknowledge discomfort or defeat.

Her eyes, which moments ago had been fiery with determination were glazed now with passion, darkened with arousal. Walker lowered his gaze to her lips, which were soft and bruised from his. Suddenly he wanted to take that lovely mouth again, this time with softness . . . with tenderness. He wanted that despite what he knew was right. And wrong.

As he stared down at her, her already flushed cheeks warmed more. He wouldn't have considered himself a man who thought in terms of "if only," but now, with her in his arms and responsive, with her hair tumbling wildly around her shoulders and her hips pressed against his, he wished they'd met at a different time or had been different people. He wished too that he didn't have one disastrous marriage under his belt and that she didn't insist on interfering with how he raised his daughter. The list could go on, and still he would stand here with nothing changed. Wishing was for fools.

Walker tightened his hold on her. Everyone deserved a few minutes of foolishness in their life. "I want to make love."

She wanted that too. It was all she'd been able to think of for days. "No," she said, her voice barely a whisper.

He shifted his gaze back to hers, acknowledging that to stop would be one of the hardest things he'd ever done. "Don't say that unless you mean it, Alex," he murmured, straightening but not loosening his hold on her. "Because if you ask me to, I will."

"A Boston-bred gentleman to the end." She

tried to laugh, the sound husky and breathless, more passion than mirth.

"Last chance, Alex."

She stared into his dark, sultry eyes. She burned with wanting him, yet she would protect herself instead. "Yes . . . stop."

Walker lifted his lips in a small smile. "No," he returned, already lowering his mouth to hers. As he'd wanted, this time he caressed her mouth with his, coaxing hers . . . seducing hers. He rubbed his lips lightly against hers, then nipped at the corners of her mouth, at her full bottom lip.

As he slowed and softened, he noticed things he hadn't in his frenzy—the clean, woodsy scent of her shampoo, the way the cowl neck of her wool sweater tickled his chin and, surprisingly, that she tasted of chocolate. Pleased, he smiled against her lips—the health nut had succumbed to the worst treat of them all.

She felt his smile and sagged against him. She didn't worry that he was laughing at her, she knew he wasn't. Instead the curving of his lips against hers made her feel tender toward him. It was as if, instead of only passion, they had shared something more of themselves, had made themselves ultimately vulnerable.

She should be furious that he'd tricked her, furious that he'd ignored her wishes. But his mouth was doing things to her that made her forget anger, made her forget her own mind. She smiled back.

He slid his hands down her back until he cupped her, and she caught her breath as he fitted himself to her. Gone were thoughts of vulnerabilities, gone was the ability to be lighthearted.

The same moment she grasped how badly he wanted her, he released her.

His move was unexpected, and she stumbled backward. She stared at him, angling her chin up as she realized who had ended the embrace and how ridiculous she looked. If he'd been out to prove she wanted him beyond reason, he had. But he had wanted her just as badly. The thought was comforting, and she straightened her spine. "You lied," she snapped when she'd caught her breath. "You said you'd stop."

"I did, just not right away." He caressed her cheek, which was hot and flushed under his fingers. "Besides, you're the one who lied. I listened to your eyes . . . and your body. They told me the last thing you wanted me to do was stop. The message hasn't changed."

She jerked her head away, angry at what he said, but more, that he could read her so well. Nothing would be solved by evasion, yet right now she didn't have the fortitude for emotional honesty. "This was a mistake. Please leave."

He narrowed his eyes, unreasonably annoyed by her words. "I agree. But we still have some unfinished business."

"Oh?" Her legs felt like pudding, and she wished for a chair. She folded her arms across her chest, hoping to steady herself.

"Lacy. Leave her alone."

The blood rushed to her cheeks. Nothing had changed. He was no more open or trustful than the morning they'd met. The truth of that was like a slap in the face. "Someday you're going to have to put aside your fears, Walker. If you don't, neither of you will ever be well."

Now it was his turn to ignore. He turned and

walked to the door. There, he stopped and glanced back at her. "Look who's talking, Alex. Maybe you better take a little of your own advice."

Feeling as if he'd delivered a blow to her solar plexus, Alex watched him leave the shop.

Lacy was fine. No, better than fine—wonderful. Walker stared at his daughter, relief warring with shock. She stood before him flushed with confidence and excitement. Her shirt was partially untucked, her white sandals scuffed and muddied. Her hair, in wild disarray, added to her exuberant appearance. She bore little resemblance to the shy child he'd arrived with.

"I did it, I actually did it!" She threw her arms wide. "It was so neat, Dad!"

Walker pulled her to him for a bear hug. "I'm glad you're home, Muffin. I was worried." If she noticed the way he trembled she would know just how worried he'd been. "Were you scared?"

She looked up at him. "Terrified! I really thought they'd think I was weird and not like me anymore."

"Because you'd never ridden a minibike before?" He tenderly smoothed her hair away from her cheek, then, reluctantly, let her go. "Those girls seem to be nicer than that."

"Not that, Dad. I was worried that when I told them I'm a . . . a narcoleptic, they wouldn't like me anymore."

"You told them about your narcolepsy?"

She nodded solemnly. "Yup. Do we have any more of those great chocolate cookies?"

Walker stared at her, too stunned to answer. "What made you decide that?"

"Alex suggested I do it. After all, what would they have thought if I'd just stopped my bike and went to sleep? Then they'd really have thought I was a geek!" She giggled as she dug in the cupboard for the bag of cookies. She found them, peeked inside to reassure herself there were enough to make it worth her while, then turned toward the refrigerator.

Walker watched as she poured herself a glass of milk, feeling a rush of pride at her courage. Tracy and Tina's opinion meant a lot to her, probably more than he could ever imagine. "What did you say?" he finally asked.

She shrugged as she took a long swallow of her milk. "I told them I had this thing where I get real sleepy and have to rest my eyes a lot. I told them not to worry, that they couldn't catch it. Then, I acted like it was no big deal just like Alex told me to." She stuffed a whole cookie into her mouth, then tried to talk around it. Walker was too astonished to reprimand her. "Boy was my stomach upset. I was afraid I was going to throw up."

She turned around, munching on the cookie in her mouth, another in each hand. She looked irrepressibly ten years old. Walker laughed, thinking of miracles and simultaneously of Alex. He laughed again. "Well, Muffin, it seems I don't need to worry about you quite as much as I do."

She swallowed, then smiled. "Great! Can I go with Trace and Tina to see the fireworks display tonight?"

"I'll go with" jumped to his lips, he swallowed it. Every instinct told him not to allow her to go, but he ignored them. Walker took a deep breath. He had to let her try; he had to let her grow up.

"Where and—" he cleared his throat "—and what time would you be home?"

Three days later, after he watched Lacy go off with her friends for the umpteenth time, he had to admit the truth—all his worries had proved unfounded. Lacy was flourishing with her new freedom, and other than a few sleep attacks that her friends had taken in stride, there had been no catastrophes or near disasters.

Alex had been right.

He closed the door as the three girls disappeared from sight. Lacy not only seemed happier, she seemed better. No, she *was* better. She hadn't had a cataplexic spell in days and her sleep attacks had become much less frequent.

Which, again, brought him back to Alex. Lacy had seen her, but he hadn't. He frowned and closed his eyes. He'd missed her. She'd brought sunshine and laughter into his life and he'd done nothing but deny it was there.

He opened his eyes and stared out the window. It was a beautiful fall morning, cool and crisp with just enough of a breeze to stir the fallen leaves. The forecast predicted more of the same for the next few days.

And here he sat, just as he had every morning since their argument. Missing her—her smile as well as her touch. And just as he had for days running, he told himself to go to her, apologize for being such a horse's hind end and . . .

That's where he ran into trouble. He had no problem admitting he'd been wrong. Stupid male pride was just that—stupid. But the thing he wanted to do next—pull her into his arms and kiss her senseless—he couldn't allow himself to do.

Walker stood and crossed to the sliding-glass

doors. A month ago he had boldly decided that he and Alex would become lovers, today he stood here afraid to go to her for fear he would touch her.

He shook his head. His feelings had changed. Now, making love with Alex wouldn't be just for fun or a way to relieve his physical ache. A month ago he'd been blind. A month ago he hadn't realized he could grow to care for another woman.

But he could. Facing Victoria again, oddly, had shown him that. But she'd also reminded him of all the reasons he couldn't risk it.

Walker slipped his hands into the back pockets of his jeans. Even if he could remain totally uninvolved and have a physical relationship with her, Alex wouldn't give herself lightly, she would expect more. Not necessarily marriage, but a promise to share a part of his life and heart.

They couldn't be friends—the chemistry between them was too strong. He turned away from the sunny day, smiling wryly to the empty cottage. All the noble intentions he might have now—when he couldn't see her or smell the fragrance of her perfume or hear the sweetness of her laughter—would fly out the window after five minutes in the same room with her.

But he did want to apologize. He felt he owed her a "you were right and I was wrong." He wanted to tell her thank you.

Coming to a decision, Walker checked his watch. It was Saturday; it was still early. He grabbed his car keys. He would say his piece, then leave. Five minutes, tops, and he would be out of there.

He headed out the door, praying he would catch her at home.

Eight

Alex answered the door as he lifted his hand to knock for the second time. Heart thundering in his chest, Walker stared at her. She stood in the doorway, wearing a huge pink sweater and a pair of equally pink tights. She'd pulled woolly socks on over the tights, her hair tumbled in fiery disarray around her shoulders. Her face was completely stripped of cosmetics, the tip of her nose was red.

She was the most beautiful woman he'd ever seen.

Walker stuffed his hands into his pockets. She looked surprised, and not entirely pleased, to see him. He didn't know whether to feel regret or relief. "Alex." He tried to smile.

She didn't make the same effort. Instead, she fixed her gaze evenly on his. "Hello, Walker."

If the Benjamin Franklin-style spectacles perched on her rosy nose and the book she held in her right hand were any indication, she'd been reading. "Can I come in?"

She paused, nodded, then stepped aside. As she closed the door behind them, the neckline of her sweater slipped, revealing one creamy shoulder. Walker sucked in a sharp breath as awareness cannonballed into him.

He cleared his throat and told himself to keep his eyes on her face. He did, but it didn't help—then he found himself unable to concentrate on anything but her mouth. It was the same soft shade as the flowers in the windowbox outside his bedroom. They bloomed in the spring and had a subtle but unforgettable fragrance.

Cursing flowers and fragrances and lips that were gently parted and full of sensual promise, he dragged his gaze back to hers. "Lacy and her friends went to the movies." When he mentioned his daughter's name, Heinz whined and thumped his tail against the floor. Alex wasn't as loquacious; she didn't respond at all. She didn't even blink. She wasn't going to make this easy for him. "Something starring Mel Gibson," he added. "Tracy called him a total hunk."

Her silence was unnerving. Uncomfortable, he looked around the cabin. He'd promised himself he would say his piece and leave. He could have done that five times over already. The truth was, leaving was the last thing he wanted to do. He looked back at her. "Sorry about your cold?"

Alex drew her eyebrows together. "Cold?"

He tapped the end of his own nose. "Red."

"Oh." She started to bring her hand to her face, then dropped it. "A real tearjerker," she said, motioning to her book. "Everybody dies." She crossed to the couch, praying he wouldn't notice how badly her legs shook.

Alex stared at the book for a moment, then laid

it carefully on the worn, blue upholstery. She'd hoped she could avoid this, she'd begun to believe she wouldn't have to face him again. But here he was and she didn't have the faintest idea of what to do or say or how to act.

How could she? She'd never been in love before.

The truth of that stole her breath. She hadn't realized, until this moment she hadn't been sure. Now she understood why she'd been on the brink of tears lately, why she had the feeling of being lost.

Alex squeezed her eyes shut for one moment of weakness, then turned to face him, folding her arms across her chest. They had no future, she wouldn't allow herself to agonize over this. She was better off without him. "Why are you here, Walker?"

"I wanted to talk."

"I thought we'd talked enough at our last meeting."

"You're right to be angry—"

"I'm not angry." She tossed her head, furious.

"—I acted like a real jerk."

"I won't argue with that." But that was only part of why she was angry, she thought, crossing to one of the windows and looking out at the sunshine-soaked day. She was furious at him for acting like a jerk, but more at herself. Against everything she knew was smart and safe, knowing all his faults, she'd fallen in love with him.

She watched as a squirrel scampered up the maple tree outside her window. The truth was, she could live with his bit of arrogance, his occasional single-mindedness, in fact, all his faults but one—his inability to let go of his anger at his ex-wife. She couldn't watch it eat away at him.

He couldn't truly love her as long as he was so filled with hate.

Walker stared at her stiff back and rigid shoulders and wondered at the ache in his chest. Seconds ticked past. He wished she would look at him, willed it even, but she didn't. As the silence grew, the ache grew, changed. He wanted to hold her, soothe her. He wanted to appease his own ache with her touch, wanted to make her burn for him with his. He didn't care about the consequences—he couldn't leave without touching her. Just once. Then he would go.

"Look at me, Alex." When she didn't, he murmured, "I wouldn't have guessed you to be a coward. Was I wrong?"

She met his gaze then, her eyes defiant, angry. "You wanted to talk, so talk."

He took a step toward her, then another, closing the distance between them, stopping when nothing more than a few inches of air separated them. "Yes, I came here to talk; I still will." He cupped her face in his palms. Her skin was warm, almost hot, beneath his, but she held herself absolutely still. "But first," he said slowly, gravely, "I'm going to kiss you."

Alex stood transfixed. Her brain told her to move, her heart wouldn't let her. Only her mouth seemed able to obey her commands, and even then she sounded weak-willed and breathless. "Walker, let me go."

"I promised myself I wouldn't touch you," he continued as if she hadn't spoken, trailing his thumbs across her cheekbones. Her skin was smooth, the sprinkling of freckles irresistible. "I promised I'd say what I needed to, then leave. I don't make promises lightly." He lowered his eyes from hers to her mouth. "It seems that when it comes to you my word isn't much good."

He took her lips then, and Alex fought to keep from responding. His touch, his taste, his scent tumbled over her in a sensory kaleidoscope. She ached to hold him, but curled her fingers into her palms until her nails bit into her own flesh. A moan of pleasure rose to her lips; she held it back until she was lightheaded from lack of oxygen. Just when she could hold back no longer, he released her.

Alex looked at him, but this time he turned away from her. He crossed to the door, then stopped. "You were right, Alex," Walker said, his voice thick. "Lacy needed some room, some freedom. You've seen her, you know how much happier she is, how much more confident."

He drew a deep breath and looked at his hands, then back at her. "I overreacted about the minibike thing, but I acted the only way I could—then. I was scared, Alex. Of Lacy getting hurt, but more of losing her." He paused, putting his words together carefully, finding this one of the more difficult things he'd ever done. "I think, on some level, I was trying to keep her a child . . . because she's all I have."

Alex's hands trembled and she clasped them in front of her. It hurt, standing there and pretending his words weren't carving into her. She squeezed her eyes shut. How could she have fallen in love with him? How?

"Goodbye, Alex."

She opened her eyes to see him open the door and step through it. She felt as if her legs might buckle beneath her. The door closed behind him and she pictured him crossing first the porch, then the drive. She saw him opening his car door, climbing inside, and driving out of her life forever. Her heart leapt to her throat.

"Walker!" Panicked, she raced across the room and jerked the cabin door back open. He'd reached the Mercedes and was about to climb inside. "Walker!" she cried again.

He stopped and turned to her. Alex knew she looked like a maniac but didn't care. "When are you leaving?" she asked with a breathlessness caused more by fear than a sprint across the room.

"Soon."

"What does that mean?" She pushed the hair away from her face. "Two days? Two weeks?"

"Four weeks, maybe six. Lacy's happy here, but I can't stay here indefinitely. Lacy has to go back to school."

Alex pressed the flat of her hand against her stomach. "You won't ever come back, will you?"

Walker met her gaze evenly. "Probably not."

She looked away, then back, anger creeping into her tone. "Why did you come here today? Why didn't you just go?"

"Maybe I should have, but"—he paused—"I couldn't leave things the way they were between us."

"It wouldn't have mattered." She angled her chin up. "I was just some bizarre woman you met in Arkansas. A meaningless flirtation."

Her words were like a fist to his chest. "No, Alex, it would have mattered. I don't think of you—wouldn't think of you—that way."

A trembling sensation started in the pit of her stomach and traveled upward. "Why?"

He stared at her for long moments. "I care about you."

Lightheaded, Alex leaned back against the doorframe. She drew in three deep breaths in an attempt to steady herself. The oxygen affected her not at all. "I care about you too," she whispered. "Too much."

The wind sighed through the trees, an acorn hit the top of Walker's car with a crack. Behind her, Heinz whined in his sleep. But neither she or Walker moved a muscle. It was as if there was an invisible energy field between them, holding them transfixed.

Finally, Alex broke the connection. She looked down at her feet, then back up at him. She was scared to death—even her toes were quivering. She faced him. "What should we do about this?"

Twenty feet separated them. He wanted to touch her, his fingers itched to do so. He didn't move a muscle. "You tell me."

Alex's breath caught. He stood beside his big, expensive car, the breeze ruffling his dark hair. He looked tired, drawn. Her heartstrings tugged, her pulse fluttered. She suspected she, not Lacy, was responsible for his sleeplessness. He held himself rigidly, but his eyes were soft and somehow wistful—like those of a child on Christmas morning.

Alex pressed harder against the doorframe until the wood bit into her back. Dear Lord, she'd never guessed love would hurt like this! It squeezed her until she was robbed of her breath as well as her good sense.

But with the absence of good sense came lassitude. The future would take care of itself—today was for living. Tomorrow would be too late.

She met his gaze evenly, without question. There would be no regrets later, no second-guessing herself. She wanted this; she wanted him. Soon he would be gone. "Come back inside, Walker."

Without waiting for him, she moved through the doorway and into the cabin.

Walker hesitated, but only a moment. He closed the distance between them, found her standing in the center of the room. She seemed too vulnerable standing there in her oversize pink sweater and little girl tights, and the hesitation he hadn't felt the moment before barreled over him. He had to tell her the truth. "I can't make you any promises . . . I can't give you a commitment."

"I don't expect any." As he opened his mouth to protest, she stopped him. "We're from two different worlds, but more importantly, two different perspectives. You told me weeks ago you like things to make sense, you like all the pieces to fit together. We don't, Walker. We're so ill-fitting it's laughable that we should be standing here like this. But still, there's . . . something between us. Something we can't deny, even though we've both tried."

She lowered her head for a moment, her red hair tumbled forward, hiding her face. When she looked back at him, her eyes were bright, her cheeks flushed. She was so beautiful she took his breath away.

"It's not me I'm worried about," Walker said softly. "I know how I feel." He took a step forward, then stopped. "What about you, Alex? What do you want?"

"I'm not sure what I want matters." She shook her head. "I don't believe in accidents or fate.

There's an order to the universe, a rhyme or reason for everything."

"And for us?"

"I don't know. For me, the belief is enough. All I ask is that you be honest with me."

He smiled, wryly. "We haven't been so far."

"No, not so far." Alex hooked her fingers under the hem of her sweater and lifted it slowly over her head. She wasn't wearing a bra, and her nipples puckered in response to the chill room. Squaring her shoulders, she tossed the garment aside. "Honesty," she said softly.

Arousal was swift and stunning. Walker worked to catch his breath, but more, he struggled for control. She stood before him, slim and strong and proud, offering herself to him simply and without artifice. Her skin was the color of fresh cream; her breasts were small, round, and perfect.

They seemed to beg for his hands.

He caught the hem of his own sweater. "Honesty," he repeated, just as softly, his voice thick with need. He moved toward her, yanking the garment over his head, tossing it aside. He wore an oxford-cloth shirt underneath, he began unbuttoning it. When he reached her, his chest was as naked as hers.

They stood, barely touching. With each breath, the peaks of her breasts brushed him. Walker sucked in his own breath at the exquisite torture.

"Come." Alex caught his hand and led him toward the ladder that led to her loft.

They climbed the ladder, not speaking, not touching. There were windows up there as well. Sunlight streamed through them, bathing the bed in a brilliant white light. It also streamed through the faceted pieces of quartz that lined the sill; on the single pillow there was reflected one small but perfect rainbow.

Like Alex, there was something at once innocent and bewitching about the bedroom. Something that invited, warmly and with open arms. In that moment Walker had the sense that once inside he would never want to leave, and he thought about running.

But he didn't run. Instead, he turned to her and cupping her face in his hands, he lowered his mouth to hers. Her lips were waiting, open to him, her tongue ready. He brushed his mouth against hers, touched her tongue with his own, then retreated, all the while being careful, being in control.

Alex felt his caution, sensed his need for control. She would have him without his props, without control this first time. She wanted him to plunge into her with the same ferocity that clawed at her. No excuses, no rational words—the mindlessness that happens when the heart and senses completely override the intellect.

She clutched at him, pressed herself against him, but still he held back. With a sound of frustration, she pulled away. "Don't make me wait, Walker."

He dragged his fingers through her hair, pulling her back to him. "I want to go slow . . . to make it good for you—"

"No, not for me." She arched her neck to meet his eyes. "That's not what I want."

It was all he could do to form the words. "What do you want, Alex?"

"You already know—honesty." In the confines of the tiny loft, they were almost on top of each other. She moved closer. She put her hand between them. He was hard and aching. He was ready. She heard his sharply indrawn breath, felt his abdominal muscles tighten. "If you were totally uncivilized, what would you do now?"

Walker closed his hands over her breasts—they seemed to swell to fill him. Her hardened nipples pressed against his palms even as she moved her own fingers. He heard her breathing quicken—or was that his own?

The last of his control snapped. He pressed his mouth to her ear, his voice harsh with need. "I would lay you on the bed and enter you quickly, almost roughly. Then, when I could breathe, I would make love to you . . . so slowly, so exquisitely that you would beg me to take you. But still I would make you wait."

Her head fell back; he plundered the fragrant flesh of her neck. His breath was ragged, hers quick. He bit, she clawed, they toppled to the bed.

Her tights clung, and Walker tore at them. He was too slow with the snap and zipper to his jeans, she shoved his fingers aside.

Walker groaned, dizzy with desire and freedom. It was the way it'd been when they'd kissed—he felt young and strong and fearless. The way he had before disillusionment. Before Victoria. Now, there was no reason to second-guess himself, no reason to worry over the past or the future. Everything would take care of itself; life was simple. As simple as a sigh, a caress, a murmured plea.

Alex wrapped her legs around him as he plunged into her. He was hers. No props or pretenses. Neither of them was in control, there was nothing to be won or lost. There was only two people and one, unrestrained passion.

And love. Alex tightened her legs and caught his mouth, sensation after sensation barreling over and through her. At this moment, she had enough love for them both.

She cried out then, digging her fingers into his back, arching her own back in ecstasy. He was with her, not a heartbeat of time were they off. It was as if they were made for each other.

Later, damp and panting, they held each other, not speaking but not self-consciously quiet either. The silence was broken by the occasional squawk of a bird, by the sound of Heinz moving around downstairs, by the rustle of the bedclothes.

Alex made a sound of contentment and smiled to herself as she trailed a finger over Walker's muscled chest. Earlier she'd been shocked by how love could hurt, now she understood. There couldn't be spring without fall, life without death, one dramatic force without another on the opposite end of the spectrum. And on the opposite end from that debilitating pain was a feeling of such joy, of being so full, so complete, so . . . utterly happy.

Under her fingers she felt his heartbeat, sure, steady, but still too fast. Alex placed a kiss over the place, then nipped, her smile widening as he complained.

"That hurt, witch." He dragged her up, so their faces were level. Her red hair was wild from their passion and he grinned—she really did look like the witch he'd called her. But not the kind with warts who frightened children. The kind that seduced men, then stole their souls. He wondered if she hadn't stolen his.

Pushing that uncomfortable thought away, he

mock growled. "We have some unfinished business, lady."

He had said the same thing to her days before. She knew that now he meant something totally different. She cocked her head. "Is that so?"

"Mmm-hmm." He caught her mouth, but after one teasing taste, released it.

She playfully pouted. "I seem to remember something about making slow, exquisite love."

He ran the flat of his hand over the curve of her hip, then lower. "Funny . . ." He trailed his fingers over her thigh, then dipped between them. She gasped, and he smiled. "What I remember is a promise . . . something about making you beg."

His fingers were working magic on her. Her head fell back even as the breath shuddered past her lips. "Never."

He ignored her. But he also denied her, lifting his hands once again to her hair. "Do you know—" he tangled his fingers in the silky stuff, the color so brilliant he could imagine it actually put off heat—"I wondered, for just a moment when we first met, if you dyed your hair." At her indignant sound, he laughed. "Shocking isn't it, especially considering . . ." He let his gaze wander from the top of her head, to her equally fiery eyebrows and lashes, then lower to the point where her thighs met. He tangled his gaze with hers once again. "You're terribly consistent, Alex."

She blushed and he laughed, taking his mouth over the path his eyes had traveled moments before. Her skin was like warmed cream, sweet and smooth, she smelled feminine but natural, like wildflowers and woods. Walker stopped every so often to nuzzle and nip, enjoying the way her skin quivered under his ministrations and the way she moaned his name.

"Begging already?" he teased, lifting up on an elbow so he could drink in her passion-flushed features. "I'm better than I thought."

Alex narrowed her eyes. "More conceited you mean."

He pressed his mouth to the soft spot just below her navel and teased it with his lips, tongue, and teeth. As her muscles tightened under his sensual attack, he laughed and looked back up at her. "No, not at all."

She shifted out of his grasp. "I promise you, I'll not beg."

He caught her again. "And I promise you you will."

She smiled saucily, tangling her fingers in his thick, dark hair. "Maybe the one who cries out will be you," she murmured, then caught his mouth.

The war of eros was on. He worked to keep his promise, she to keep hers. Alex stroked her tongue against his, imitating the motions with her body. He was hard and angular, she gentle curves; his flesh was firm, muscled, and lightly furred, hers soft, smooth, and perfumed. She reveled in their differences, pleasured in the contrast of textures and scents and tastes.

Alex caught her bottom lip between her teeth, determined not to moan her pleasure. He did things with his hands she hadn't dreamed possible—moving his fingers in slow, wicked circles, finding places she'd before thought ordinary and unremarkable. The only thing unremarkable was that she'd lived so long without him. Again a wave of pleasure rolled over her; still she didn't cry out

Walker breathed in the fragrance that was wholly Alex and totally female and felt his determination slipping. He ached for her, ached in a way that was almost frightening in its intensity—it was an ache of physical desire, but more, one of softness and need and possessiveness.

He opened his eyes. The sun had changed angles and the reflected rainbow lay directly over Alex's heart. His own heart did a funny, little lurch. And in that moment, he thought about stopping, about kissing her good-bye, getting dressed, and walking out of her life forever. Then she opened her eyes and smiled at him, and he knew it was too late. It had been too late for a long time.

Walker could wait no longer and rolled onto his back, pulling her over and onto him. Alex went willingly, making sounds of pleasure and approval as she sank onto him. They moved together, she telling him what she needed and he responding to those needs. She did the same for him.

So in the end neither won, and both won. She fell against him, without breath and totally spent.

They lay that way, with Alex sprawled on top of him, her face burrowed into his shoulder, his arms holding her tightly, for longer than Walker could fathom. Seconds became minutes, minutes grouped together to form time passing. Walker stroked her hair, loving the way it felt against his skin, the way the strands slithered through his fingers.

Her breath whispered rhythmically against his flesh, and he thought she slept. Possessively, he tightened his arm around her. He'd done what he knew he shouldn't have. Even though he wanted to offer her everything, he could offer her nothing. He drew his eyebrows together. And the truth was, he wasn't sure who would hurt more when he left.

She sighed and stirred and opened her eyes. "Walker?" she murmured, seeing his frown.

His expression cleared. "You're awake."

"Mmm-hmm." She resisted the urge to clutch at him. He was regretting their making love; she saw it in the frown, heard it in his voice, sensed it in the tightness of his body. She inched off him. "You okay?"

"Yeah." He pulled her back into his side, feeling cold and somehow lost without her against him. "I don't imagine you're hungry?"

She tipped her face up to his, relieved. "Then you imagine wrong—I'm starved!"

He forced a smile. "Think you can whip up something that's only semihealthy?"

She arched her eyebrows indignantly. "*Me* whip up? Your true character is showing."

He laughed. "I showed my true character already, and I haven't the energy to do it again."

"Chauvinist—"

"Pig," he finished for her, laughing as she threw aside the covers. He caught her leg as she started to slip out of the bed and leaning over, nipped her calf. "We could order out—anyone deliver to the middle of nowhere?"

Alex sniffed. "You'd think a man who could make it through medical school could learn his way around a kitchen!" She wagged her index finger at him. "I'll cook, but you must promise to lavish me with attention while I do. And no cracks about the results!"

He held up two fingers. "Doctor's honor."

"Now you really will make me laugh."

She slid out of bed then and crossed the room for her robe. Smiling, Walker leaned back against the pillows folding his arms behind his head. When she bent to pull her sweat socks on, he whistled like a sailor on leave, knowing it would infuriate her. "Hey, baby," he called, making smacking noises.

Alex glared at him, pink easing up her cheeks. She yanked on her other sock. "Knock it off, Walker."

He whistled again. "Sexy mama, why don't you come over here and get a taste of a real man. If you play your cards right, I'll give you a glimpse of paradise."

Alex grinned and trailed her gaze insolently over him. He'd left himself open. "Hey, baby . . . sure you're man enough?" With that, she tossed his pants at him. They hit him in the chest. "Show's over, cowboy. Meet me downstairs."

She descended the ladder to the sound of his appreciative laughter.

Forty minutes later they sat down at Alex's tiny kitchen table to eat. The tabletop was scarred and the chairs mismatched, but the food was delicious. They feasted on angel hair pasta smothered in sweet basil tomato sauce and a tossed salad, made with a variety of the freshest fall produce. The sauce had only needed defrosting and Walker had been able to throw together the salad with a minimum of supervision. They shared the last of a bottle of sparkling grape juice as the sun began to set.

This would be terribly romantic, Alex thought, if only Walker would say something. She forced herself to bring her fork to her mouth. What was he thinking? Why wouldn't he look at her?

Suddenly, she set down her fork, unable to eat another bite. She cleared her throat. He didn't look up. If she didn't break this silence, she would go crazy. "When you're a vegetarian, you have to learn to cook or you'll starve. You can't just throw a steak under the broiler."

"I'm sure," Walker murmured, looking up only, it seemed to her, as an afterthought. "And everything's great, Alex. Just great."

Her heart sank both at the platitude and his return to silence. "Thanks," she muttered, returning her own attention to her plate.

The rest of the meal passed as the beginning had, in total, depressing quiet. Still toying with her food, she sneaked a peek at him and her spirits sank further. She'd been right before, he regretted their making love. He wished he was anywhere but here and was ruing the day they met.

Alex lifted her chin. Well, she would have her tongue cut out before she'd ever invite him into her bed again. *Right, Alex,* she scolded herself, her cheeks heating, *you would have him again this minute if he asked.*

He didn't ask. Instead, he laid down his fork and checked his watch. "Lacy's sure to be home by now."

"You better go then." Alex stood and began clearing the table.

"Let me," Walker said, following her to her feet. "I didn't mean to imply I had to run out the door."

"That's okay. You're right, Lacy's probably wondering where you are."

He gently pushed her hands aside and finished clearing the table, then dried the dishes as she washed them. When that was done, he placed a quick kiss on her lips. "I hate to leave."

"Right." She started toward the door.

He followed, grabbing her elbow when she reached the door. "What's that supposed to mean?"

Without subtlety, she extricated herself from his grasp, then folded her arms across her chest. "What do you think?"

Walker narrowed his eyes. "I don't know. Why don't you tell me?"

"I won't see you again, will I?"

He stared at her, shocked. "Alex, where did that come from?"

"You promised me honesty and right now you're being pretty damn dishonest." She glared at him, willing herself not to cry. "The moment your head cleared you were out that door!"

"Talking about honesty—" Walker shifted his gaze to the couch, then looked back at her. "What about that book?"

"What about it?"

"It's a book on herb gardening, Alex." His tone was gentle. "Why were you crying earlier?"

She'd been crying over him. She suspected he knew that. "None of your damn business!" Angry, she tossed her head back to look at him. "You're trying to change the subject. Admit it."

He shook his head. "That's not true, Alex."

She let her breath out in an angry huff. "You don't say two words to me during our meal, then you run out the door immediately afterward. Are you telling me this is how men show they're having a great time and don't want to leave?"

"Get dressed, Alex. We're going out to dinner."

"We just ate."

Walker groaned. "That's not the point. We'll have drinks then, or dessert. I want to be with you."

"I understand that you have plans—"

"I don't have plans!" He hauled her against his chest. "I was quiet through the meal because I was preoccupied. Not because I wished I was anywhere else or was regretting becoming your lover. A lot has happened in the last couple of hours and . . ." His words trailed off and he drew a deep breath. "Alex, you're coming with me whether you want to or not."

She curled her fingers into his soft, ivory sweater. He'd called himself her lover, they were lovers. She smiled, just a little, she couldn't help herself. "Why's that?"

"So you don't think what you're obviously thinking." He tightened his arms. "I repeat, I *don't* regret this afternoon. I *don't* feel uncomfortable, and I'm *not* trying to escape."

He'd punctuated each word with a kiss, and now she was lightheaded, totally convinced but not ready to step out of his arms. "I wouldn't want to force you—"

"Dammit, Alex! I want you with me! Now are you going to get dressed or do you want Lacy and her friends to see you in your robe?"

From the tone of his voice, Alex knew his was not an idle threat. She ran upstairs and dressed as quickly as she could.

Nine

Four weeks, Alex thought, watching as Walker scooped his sleeping daughter out of the back seat of the car. She couldn't believe four weeks had passed since she and Walker had become lovers.

But they had—she was still dizzy from them. It had been four weeks filled with laughter and lovemaking, moonlight strolls and deep discussions. They'd found that despite their obvious and drastic differences, they had a lot in common, from likes and dislikes to views on raising children and religion.

Alex drew her eyebrows together as she hurried to open the cottage door for him. But there were things they would never agree on, things about her he would never be able to accept.

She was an empath. That wouldn't change, not ever.

She swung the door open and their eyes met. As they did something passed between them, something strong and warm and electric; Alex felt the connection down to the tips of her toes. In that moment she could believe that all problems were resolvable. Then he turned and started down the hall toward the girl's bedroom and she was left alone and shivering in the open doorway.

Alex shut the door and fastened the chain lock. Still shivering, she went to the kitchen to make some tea. She put a kettle of water on and took out the tea and two mugs. Walker would be some time. He would tuck Lacy in, then as was his habit, he would watch her sleep for a few minutes to make sure she was comfortable and sleeping deeply.

Then he would come to her and they would make love.

Her stomach dropped to her toes, as it always did when she thought of being in Walker's arms, of being his lover.

She peered at her reflection in the window above the sink, pulling her fingers through her hair, fluffing it. He loved her hair—loved to let it whisper over his flesh, loved to bury his face in it. He told her it felt like silk and looked like fire. He made her feel beautiful and sensuous and totally female.

She dropped her hands. How would she feel when he was gone?

Even as she tried to push the question away, she drew her eyebrows together, remembering that day so many weeks ago and the question she had asked him.

"When are you leaving?"

"Four weeks," he had answered. "Maybe six."

That was now. Tomorrow she would be living on borrowed time. She lowered her eyes from the image of herself to her trembling hands. She clasped them together. And tomorrow he could leave and she wouldn't have the right, not really, to be surprised. Or upset.

But she would be. By some unspoken agreement, she and Walker never discussed the future, whether it was the next day, the next week, or forever. Each morning she woke up fearful that he wouldn't call, that she wouldn't see him; each day her fears proved unfounded.

Alex tightened her fingers until her nails bit into her palms. One day he wouldn't call or stop by, one day he and Lacy would go back to Boston. And her heart would splinter into a billion irreparable pieces.

The kettle whistled, and Alex poured the water over the tea bags. Immediately the aroma of fruit and almonds wafted up to her. Tears sprang to her eyes but she blinked them away. Walker was a generous, considerate lover. Not just in bed— where he was astounding—but in every other part of their relationship as well. He brought her all the traditional gifts like flowers and candy, but it was the not-so-traditional ones that wrenched her heart—fresh produce for the many vegetarian dishes she made and he ate without complaint, spectacularly colored leaves he found and pressed for her, shiny or unusually shaped rocks. Alex drew in the aroma of the tea once again. And in his cottage he had stocked all her favorite things, including this herb tea. Her favorite flavor.

She wrapped her hands around one of the steaming mugs, warming them. She wouldn't complain when he was gone, she wouldn't feel sorry for herself. The last four weeks had been wonderful. Alex smiled, staring down at the tea as it steeped. She'd never imagined lovemaking could be so exhilarating and terrifying and exhausting. How could she be so totally satiated and so unappeasably hungry at the same time? Her cheeks heated. She never got enough of him—or he of her.

If they could have, they probably would have spent all their time in bed. Alex plucked the tea bags from the cups and tossed them in the trash. But she'd had the shop to take care of and he'd had Lacy. These nighttime hours had become so precious to them. Even so, when they'd been here, she'd had to leave the warmth of his arms before Lacy awakened, or if at her place, he would have to hurry to beat his daughter home. Either way, each time she felt as if a part of her was being wrenched away.

What would it feel like when he left for good?

Her chest tightened, and she suddenly felt as if she couldn't breath. She lowered her eyes to her hands, still clutching the mug. She would know, maybe for the first time in her life, real pain.

"Lacy's down for the count. Check the refrigerator, I bought you one of your favorites."

Alex swung around just in time to catch the kiss he blew her before he ducked back out the door. A moment later she heard him fiddling with the radio and then the soft strains of a love song she remembered but couldn't place. It was a tune about an unrequited romance and had always made her sad.

Appropriate. This could be their last night together.

Alex shook her head, once again trying to push away her thoughts. She turned and opened the refrigerator. She stared into the nearly empty appliance for several seconds, relief rushing over her. He'd stocked sparkling grape juice. Not one bottle or two—but three full-size bottles.

Tonight wasn't the end. She had a little more time.

She took out one of the bottles and hugged it to her. It was chilled and ready for drinking. Three bottles. What did that mean? Three nights? Or maybe, if she drank very slowly, the juice would last a week or even two.

Alex frowned. Or maybe the number of bottles wasn't at all significant. Maybe she was only—

"What's the matter, Alex? Wrong brand?"

She looked up to find Walker watching her from the doorway. He was leaning against the doorjamb, the sleeves of his navy sweater pushed up on his forearms. He looked casual and confident and sexy as hell. Her pulse scrambled even as she met his eyes once again. By the laughter there, she suspected he'd been watching her for several moments.

But it wasn't the amusement in his dark gaze that drew her—it was the awareness. He wanted her, now, this moment, on the kitchen floor and fully clothed. He held back because he was civilized . . . and because he knew she wanted him just as badly. She cleared her throat and glanced down at the label. Two could play the waiting game. "It's perfect."

He crossed to her and took the bottle from her hands, placing it on the counter. "No," he murmured, "you're perfect."

Then he took her mouth. Their kiss was achingly slow and dizzyingly thorough. It seduced, yes, but it promised much more . . . much later. Her muscles turned to putty, she sagged against him.

He released her mouth but not her body, holding her against him as if he was afraid she would try to run away. "Do you dance?"

Alex laughed up at him, feeling as if she could dance on clouds. "I took lessons, my mother insisted. She believed a lady had to be skilled on the dance floor. I know them all, the waltz, the tango, even the cha-cha."

"The cha-cha," Walker repeated, amusement and arousal making his voice soft and thick. He lowered his head, trailing his lips along an eyebrow, her cheek, catching the last of her laughter with his mouth. "And what of the bedroom? Did she think a lady needed those skills as well?"

"Of course," she whispered, curling her fingers into the soft weave of his sweater and tipping her head to give him access to the column of her throat. His lips moved deliciously over her, pausing when he found the sensitive flesh behind her ear. Her breath caught as he nipped, then stroked with his tongue.

When she once again found her voice, she added, "Every southern woman knows the importance of bedroom wiles. We're born knowing them—we have to be, a lady would never speak of such things."

"Wiles?" Walker lifted his head and laughed, the sound deep and low in his throat. He cupped her face in his palms. "So my red-haired witch, my crystal-toting tomboy is really, down deep, Scarlett O'Hara dressed in blue jeans and hiking boots."

Feeling every bit the romantic heroine, Alex fluttered her lashes in just the way her mother had showed her when she was twelve. "Well, one can't completely escape one's heritage."

His laughter died, and he stroked his thumbs across her cheekbones, studying her. "Or one's past," he murmured, then lowered his mouth to hers. His lips clung to hers, then parted; his tongue parried, then twined with hers.

Alex pressed against him, reveling in both his touch and taste. How could she at once feel so energized and so weightless? And how from no more than the touch of his lips against hers? She knew the answer to neither question, only that she couldn't bear for the feeling to end.

Walker pulled a fraction away from her. Although their mouths, their bodies, no longer touched, his heat, his strength, still engulfed her. She opened her eyes. His were dark and filled with desire.

"I want to hold you against me," he whispered, catching her hand and bringing it to his mouth. He placed a lingering kiss in her palm, then laced his fingers through hers. "I want to dance with you, under the stars and surrounded by the black night."

His breath was warm against her cheek. "It's cold," she murmured, her voice husky. "We'll freeze."

He trailed a finger across her breasts. Her nipples tightened in response. "Body heat will keep us warm."

It would, she thought, still amazed at how he could make her feel. It could be twenty below and still he would keep her warm. She tipped her head back provocatively. "And then?"

"Then?" He tangled his fingers in her hair.

"Yes." She closed her eyes, enjoying the feeling of his hands threading through her hair. She reopened them and met his gaze evenly. "After we dance. What then?"

He laughed softly. "Do you really wonder?"

She didn't and within minutes they were on the patio, dancing under the black, star-sprinkled sky. For a long time they didn't speak, just enjoyed the moment and moving together.

Walker broke the silence first, laughing a little as he said, "You make me feel young and reckless and totally irresponsible."

Alex arched her brows. "The sensible Dr. Ridgeman? I don't believe it."

He inched her even closer and mock-growled, "Believe it, lady. Or I'll be forced to prove it."

Alex laughed lightly. "Promises, promises." She rubbed her cheek against the soft wool of his coat. It smelled like he did—of soap and spice and the night air.

Silence stretched between them once again. Walker moved his hand slowly, rhythmically up and down the center of her back. When he spoke, his voice was low and tender. "Thank you for suggesting today, Alex. It took Lacy's mind off Tracy and Tina leaving." He rubbed his chin against the top of her head. "She's never had 'best friends' before, and she was devastated when they waved good-bye."

Alex knew—she had felt the girl's turbulent emotions and had ached for her. "How's she doing now?"

"She's still upset." He paused. "She wants to go home, Alex. She told me tonight."

"Oh." Fear left a bitter taste in her mouth. Alex swallowed and dragged her gaze from his. She didn't know what he would say next but she suspected, and she pressed her face into his shoulder, childishly hoping that if she ignored the truth it would go away. It didn't.

"Alex, these last weeks have been—"

"Don't." She placed her gloved hand over his mouth. The thing she worried over all day was happening, and now she didn't want to know; she wouldn't wonder. Tomorrow or the day after that or whenever would be soon enough for reality. Tonight she wanted the dream to continue.

She stopped dancing. Still gazing up at him, she trailed her thumb across his lower lip. The beginning of his beard was rough against her palm; his breath was warm against her skin. His eyes were full of regret.

Her breath caught. "Don't," she repeated, this time referring to the emotion in his eyes. "Don't be sorry."

"I'm not." He turned his head and pressed a kiss in her palm. She shuddered and curled her fingers around his face. "I only wish—"

"No . . . no second-guessing or regrets or futile wishes." She drew in a lungful of the crisp night air. It steadied her, made her brave. "Make love to me, Walker. Carry me to your bed and make love to me until nothing exists but us and the moment. Make me forget this is good-bye."

Without a word, he swept her into his arms and carried her inside. There, he laid her across the bed and began undressing her. He moved slowly, savoring. As he peeled each garment off he found a new place to explore, to taste, a new way to make her sigh or call his name.

Alex returned the favor, pushing his coat off his shoulders, fumbling with buttons and buckle and zipper. She didn't speak, tried not to think; the time for both was long past. Now was for sensation—and making memories.

Then, finally, he was as naked as she. She ran her hands over the hard planes of his body, memorizing for later when she was alone. She followed her hands with her mouth, delighting in the way his muscles tightened, in the way he hardened, and in her own power. But not nearly powerful enough, she thought. Not enough to make him stay.

Walker caught her hands and brought them over her head. For long seconds he gazed at her. When they'd been outside there hadn't seemed to be a moon, yet now moonlight filtered through the windows, bathing her ivory flesh in cool blue light. Light and shadow described form—she was perfection.

Suddenly Walker felt as if he would die if he didn't have her, he knew she felt the same. It was in her pleading eyes, her urgent hands, in the way she undulated her hips in invitation. He gave them what they both wanted, slipping into her, murmuring her name as he did.

Alex gasped and arched, then wrapped her arms and legs around him. She held tightly and wished, wished with all her heart, that she would never have to let him go. She moved with him, faster and faster, even though she knew to do so would mean facing the inevitable—the sweet followed by the bittersweet, ecstasy followed by despair.

And then it was over. She cried out his name at the same instant he said hers, together they returned to reality to face both the moment and the future.

Tell him, she thought as she lay cuddled into

his side, listening to his runaway heart. *Tell him you love him.* She pressed her face in his side. She hadn't told him because she hadn't felt it was what either of them needed. She'd known he hadn't the capacity to return her love. But now, even though it wouldn't change a thing, she felt as if he should know, as if not to tell him would be wrong, dishonest.

She tilted her head back so she could see his face, the face she loved so much. She drew her eyebrows together. After lovemaking he usually looked sleepy and satisfied, tonight he looked pensive, even tense. "Walker?"

He met her gaze, his lazy smile didn't reach his eyes. "Hmm?"

"I want . . . I need to say something that . . ." Still uncertain if she had the courage to tell him, she drew in a deep breath, then exhaled slowly. She didn't. Nor was she sure she trusted her own motives. She would not use her love to try and make him stay. "Never mind. It wasn't important."

He searched her face with his eyes. "Something's bothering you, go ahead and—"

His words were interrupted by a scream.

Lacy.

They both bolted up, Walker grabbing his pants and yanking them on as he raced to his daughter's room, Alex paused only long enough to pull on and button her coat. When she reached the girl's bedroom, Walker was on the edge of the bed, his arms around Lacy. She was sobbing.

"It's all right, Muffin. Daddy's here."

Halfway into the room Alex stopped dead, Lacy's pains hitting her like wrecking balls. She couldn't catch her breath, and she brought a hand to her chest, panicked.

Oh, Lord . . . Oh, Lord . . . the pains had never been this intense! Even the time she'd overloaded, they hadn't been this bad. What was she . . . she had to . . . get out . . .

Alex squeezed her eyes shut, fighting the pains and the urge to run. As if from a distance, she heard Walker trying to soothe his daughter.

"It was only a dream. You're safe, Muffin."

"It was so real," the girl replied, her voice small and broken.

"Shh, it's okay now. Quiet . . ."

Alex took a step backward, the pain in her throat worsening. She felt as if she was being choked and desperately sucked in air. She stared at Walker and Lacy, heart thundering in her chest, knowing something wasn't right about the scene she was witnessing, that here was a key to Lacy's illness. If only she could think, if only . . . she could get some . . . air . . .

The panic took her then, and Alex turned and fled from the room.

Thirty minutes later she heard the patio doors slide open and knew that Lacy was asleep. She didn't turn and look at him as he crossed to her. She needed every extra second to prepare herself for what was sure to be, if not an ugly scene, a wrenching one.

Alex wrapped her arms tighter around herself. She knew now what was wrong with Lacy. To explain it to Walker she would have to tell him the truth about herself. Tomorrow had come even sooner than she'd feared.

"She's fine now," Walker murmured, stopping beside her. "Sound asleep." He looked up at the stars, rubbing his brow wearily. "She hasn't had one of those hallucinatory dreams in a while. I'd almost convinced myself they'd stopped for good."

He turned to her. "I'm sorry for the timing, sorry you had to see—" He saw that her teeth were chattering and really looked at her. "My God, Alex, you don't have any shoes on!"

She looked down at her feet in surprise. She didn't. She'd left the house without a thought for anything but escape. But more surprising, she didn't feel the cold. She was numb. "We need to talk."

He tried to pull her into his arms, she stepped away. "Don't touch me, Walker. Not now. I can't say what I have to while I'm in your arms."

"Alex?" Walker drew his eyebrows together, seeing now how pale she was. "What's wrong? Are you ill?"

"No, I'm fine." She wasn't, she felt as if she might crumble at any moment. The last thing she wanted to do was face him, yet she had to. For Lacy's sake . . . and his. She tipped her chin up and said as calmly and evenly as she could, "I understand now, Walker. I know what's wrong."

"Come back inside, Alex." He caught her hand. "It's too cold out here."

She shook her head and slipped her hand from his. She saw her own was trembling and silently swore. She'd been less affected the morning she'd told her parents she had to start living for herself. The difference was, then she'd had everything to gain . . . and now she had everything to lose. "Do you know what an empath is?"

"An empath?" he repeated, obviously confused by the direction of her thoughts.

"Yes." She looked away. "It's a person who feels another's pain." She met his gaze even though it took everything she had to do so. "I'm one, Walker. An empath. It's how I knew something was wrong with Lacy before you told me. I felt her pain"—she lifted a hand to her throat—"here"—then lowered it to her chest—"and here."

When he didn't respond, she continued, "I came out here because I couldn't get any air in there. I felt as if I was being choked, and I had to get ou . . ." She didn't finish her thought; this wasn't about her, it was about Lacy.

He was staring at her as if she'd completely lost her mind. Maybe she had. She continued anyway. "I discovered my . . . gift, when I was working at the Center for Holistic Healing in San Francisco. You've probably heard of them, they've received a lot of press lately for their successful work with cancer patients." He nodded and she continued, "I worked with Dr. Raymond Beal, the so-called guru of self-healing."

"Why didn't you tell me this before?"

"You made it clear what you thought of metaphysical healing. I didn't want to push."

A muscle jumped in his jaw. "So you kept the truth from me."

She lifted her chin. "I don't lie, Walker. Not ever. I kept some information from you, but not the truth. I was up front from the beginning about what I believe and about wanting to help Lacy."

"And now you're telling me you have the ability to feel others' pain, that you're an . . . empath."

"Yes." His tone was openly skeptical. She was disappointed but not surprised. "I'd been working at the Center for about six months when I realized something was wrong." She turned away and stared out at the wooded grounds. It was always difficult to talk about that time in her life as each time she did, she relived, in a small way, the confusion, fear, and despair that had had her reeling. "I felt ill a lot of the time, symptoms ranging from general nausea to localized pains that were often quite intense."

She laughed a little, the sound high and tight even to her own ears. "At first I thought I was sick; the doctors I saw—and I saw many—couldn't find anything wrong with me. Then I thought I was losing my mind."

Alex tipped her head back to look up at the sky, drawing in a deep, fortifying breath. If their affair hadn't already been over, it would be now. But she had to be true to herself—she'd learned that a long time ago.

She met his doubting gaze once more. "Finally, I made the connection between my patients and myself. When I was working with a patient going through chemotherapy, I'd have nausea, with a patient who had breast cancer, a sharp pain in my chest. I started noting and recording what I felt and with which patient. What really threw me is when I knew where a new patient's cancer was before I'd even looked at their chart. I was terrified, I felt like some sort of freak."

Alex dragged her hands through her hair. "A healer at the Center changed that. She told me I had a rare and special gift and that I should use it to help people."

"Then what are you doing here?" he asked quietly, an edge in his voice.

"I tried," she said, just as quietly, looking him in the eye. "But it seemed the more I used this gift, the stronger it became and . . . the more it took over my life. I couldn't deal with the pain, the physical, but more, the emotional. I became so wrapped up in my patients' lives that when one would win the battle with disease and leave I felt as if a part of me was being wrenched away. When a patient lost the battle . . . well, I can't put the way that felt into words."

He faced her, his expression as if etched in stone. She wished she could read some softness there. "So you're hiding here in the middle of nowhere."

Alex blanched. It hurt to hear him say it. It hurt because it was true. "Yes."

"What about Lacy, Alex? Why her?"

"I don't know why. I never meant to get involved with anyone here. But we met and I knew . . . I felt her pain so strongly. I couldn't ignore her cry for help."

Walker made a strangled sound, and Alex clasped her hands together. "I didn't tell you because I knew you'd react this way."

"Is that so?" He swung away from her, then back. "Is this what you were going to tell me inside, before Lacy—"

"No."

"Why are you telling me now?"

"Because of Lacy," she answered simply. "I know now what's wrong with her. Tonight the last piece of the puzzle dropped into place."

Walker went completely still, his eyes narrowing as he looked at her. "Really? But I thought we knew all along what was wrong with Lacy. She has narcolepsy."

"I'm talking about the cause, Walker. Not the symptom."

"We've been through this before."

She tossed her head back. "You didn't ask Lacy about her dream. Why?"

He stiffened. "I've asked before. She doesn't like to talk about them."

"Or is it she knows you don't like to hear about them?"

He rounded on her. "Spit it out, Alex."

"Narcolepsy is a form of escape—escaping through sleep. Any book on metaphysical healing will tell you that. I felt her pains in my throat and chest, and I knew if I could figure out why there, I would know what she was escaping—"

Walker cut her off. "I'm going inside, and if you care at all about your own health, you will too."

As he swung away from her she caught his arm. "Victoria is part of the problem. The way she treated Lacy, that she walked out. It's no coincidence that the day her friends left her, she should have one of her 'nightmares.'"

"It doesn't take a psychic to figure that out."

"I'm not a psychic," she said tightly. "I'm an empath. And I'm not finished." She paused, sucking in a deep steadying breath, then released it slowly. What she had to say next he wouldn't take well, but it had to be said anyway. "You're part of the problem, too, Walker."

He stared at her for a full ten seconds before speaking. When he did his voice was as steely as his eyes. "What did you say?"

"That you're part of Lacy's problem. Your refusal to speak of Victoria, your unwillingness to forgive her. Lacy needs to express how she feels about her mother. Don't you see . . . the pain I felt in my throat was Lacy holding back, holding everything in—*swallowing what she needed to say.*"

"Nifty," he said, practically biting the word out. "You have an explanation for your other . . . pain?"

Temper heated her cheeks, but she fought the emotion back. "The heart," she said quietly, "is the center for security and love. Lacy doesn't feel secure—her mother walked out on her, but maybe more, she's afraid if she expresses how she feels about her mother, you won't love her."

"For God's sa—"

Alex caught his hand. "Please, Walker, if you think about it it'll make sense. What have you got to lose? Talk to Lacy. Let her—"

Walker shook off her hand. "This is the biggest bunch of bunk I've ever heard! I thought I'd begun to know you. I thought my first impressions of you had been wrong. But they weren't. You're dangerous because you actually believe all this, you actually believe you can help people with this pseudo-psychiatric analysis."

He pressed the heels of his hands to his forehead as if struggling for control. A moment later, he continued. But this time his tone was colder and far more unsettling. Alex struggled with the urge to take a step back. "How dare you stand there and tell me I'm Lacy's problem. I have loved her and cared for her, I picked up the pieces when . . . she left—"

"You can't even say her name now," Alex interrupted, "four years after the fact. When are you going to let go of your anger? Lacy's mother's name was Victoria. Say it, Walker."

He balled his hands into fists. "If you want to help someone, go back to work at the clinic. We don't want your help and we didn't ask for it."

"Lacy did."

He stared at her for a moment, the emotion in his eyes feral, then he started for the door. She followed, just as furious, but more, hurt. She'd thought they'd begun to understand each other, had thought he would have been, if not understanding, at least open to her ideas. Instead, he'd tossed them all back in her face: her own personal beliefs, her belief in the kind of man he was, who she was.

By the time he reached the door she'd run in front of him, barring the way. "Forget what we shared, I'd hoped out of love for your daughter you would at least listen to what I had to say, that you would try to forgive and go on. You don't love your daughter, Walker, you only love your own belief in what is and isn't true and your own anger."

"Move, Alex, or I'll do it for you."

She stood her ground. "Earlier, I was going to tell you I'd fallen in love with you. But I realize now the man I fell in love with doesn't really exist. The man I love doesn't have a hole in his heart— a hole made by anger and an unwillingness to let go."

Walker took a step back. "What did you say?"

Alex continued as if he hadn't spoken. "When I saw you and Victoria together I knew you would never be able to love me or anyone else. Even though you didn't love her, you were too angry. Then I let emotion blind me. The blinders are off now and I have to tell you, until you make peace, Walker, until you forgive Victoria, that gaping place inside you will never heal and you'll never be happy or healthy. And the shame of it is, neither will Lacy—and she didn't do anything wrong."

She tossed her head back. "Now I'm going to

get my clothes, and if you'll let me"—her voice cracked—"I'd like to give Lacy a kiss good-bye."

Walker was silent. She didn't wait for an answer. Tears streaming down her cheeks, she did what she'd said she would and left. As she closed the door behind her, she was the one who felt as if she would never be whole again.

Ten

Walker stared out the patio doors. He felt like hell, he knew he looked worse. The day was just as miserable. It was drizzling, and the leaves that had only days before covered the ground in a colorful carpet were now soggy and brown. He sighed. Maybe they should have left yesterday.

"Dad, I'm finished packing." Lacy dragged her suitcase into the living room and dropped it near the door. She looked expectantly at her father. "What now?"

He glanced at her over his shoulder. "Did you check under your bed?"

"Yup."

He turned back to the window. "Check again."

She made a sound of exasperation and frustration. When he didn't look at her, she said "Dad?"

Walker turned at the tremulous note in his daughter's voice. He knew he'd been a bear to live with for the past week, but he hadn't been able to shake the mood. He tried to smile. He suspected it looked more like a grimace. "What, Muffin?"

"I don't want to go."

This time he made the sound of frustration. "A week ago you told me that you did. And the new school term is about to begin."

"But when I said that—" she swallowed nervously, then angled her chin up—"I thought Alex would come with us."

Walker lowered his brows even as her name rippled over him. "What made you think that?"

"I'm not a baby anymore." Lacy said, her head held high. "You guys were in love."

Walker felt as if the wind had been knocked out of him. His ten-year-old daughter had seen what he'd been too blind and stubborn to. Until it had been too late, anyway. He had too much respect for her to try to cover up the truth or deny it. He chose to ignore instead. "Go check your room again."

Lacy held her ground, her eyes defiant. "I want to see Alex."

"We already talked about this, Muffin. I don't think it's a good idea."

"Why not? She's my friend."

"Because I said so."

"That's dumb."

He stared at his daughter, feeling a bit of both pride and anxiety at the way she faced him like an adult. Besides, she was right; it was dumb. He sighed. "You can call her and say good-bye."

"What happened to make you guys break up?"

"Nothing happened. And we didn't 'break up.' It's time to go home; that's all. I have to get back to the hospital and—"

"I don't believe you." Her lower lip trembled. "I thought she was going to be my new mom. I wanted her to be!" She stamped her foot, more in an attempt, he thought, to keep from crying than from anger. "It's not fair!"

"Oh, Muffin, come here." She did and he folded her in his arms. "It hasn't been easy for you, has it?" Her face was pressed into his side but still he felt her shake her head. "I'm sorry it didn't work out. Alex is a wonderful woman, but . . ." His words trailed off. What could he tell her? That he was a jerk? And a narrow-minded, stubborn, and inflexible one at that?

He stroked his daughter's silky hair and thought of Alex. Alex with the fiery hair and infectious laugh, Alex with the heart of a tomboy and the soul of a southern belle. His chest tightened, and he squeezed his eyes shut. Would there ever come a time when he could think of her and not ache? Not quite trusting his voice, he said, "Why don't you go check your room again, then we'll go to the arcade. Okay?"

Lacy drew away from him, her eyes brimming with tears. "I don't want to go to the arcade! I want to see Alex!" She burst into tears, then ran to her room. He winced as her door slammed shut.

Damn. Walker sank into the overstuffed armchair and leaned his head back against the headrest. It seemed he handled parenting as clumsily as he handled his love life.

His love life. He rubbed a hand wearily across his forehead. A month ago he would have sworn he would never fall in love again, with Alex or anybody else. But he had. He'd fallen so hard and so fast, he hadn't even realized it had happened.

A week hadn't been much time to think, but it had been enough. What a jerk he'd been! He'd thrown away a chance for the kind of happiness everyone wanted but few ever got.

Walker jumped up and began to pace. He was too inflexible, he knew that. He was a plotter and a planner, he was comfortable with tradition. Then Alex had roared into his life and he'd had to do some major gear-shifting.

And he'd been doing admirably until she'd hit him with one too many loops at once. When she'd said she'd known how he would react to the news she was an empath, she'd been one up on him. At that moment he hadn't had any idea of how he was reacting, he'd been stunned numb.

Nor had he fully assimilated the fact that she'd worked at the Center for Holistic Healing. He'd heard of them all right, and although he wasn't convinced their methods were reliable, he had to give them credit for what they'd accomplished so far.

He stopped his pacing and once again stared out at the gloomy afternoon. Maybe he would have adjusted to both of those pieces of information if she hadn't then delivered the blow that had made him go from numb to white with rage. Even now, thinking of it was like a knife to his chest. How could *he* be part of Lacy's problem? He'd done everything he knew to be a good father; he loved her more than words could even express.

Walker pressed his fist against the cool, damp glass of the sliding door. He was lying to himself and he knew it. Was denial part of being a parent? Was the inability to see that sometimes loving or good intentions weren't enough?

His emotions had blinded him to the truth. His emotions and his prejudice. That's why Alex's words continued to claw at him. If she'd been a psychiatrist and had said the things she had, he would have been hurt and not wanted to face them—but he would have. After the first shock had passed, he would have trusted the doctor's opinion and put his own feelings aside. For Lacy's sake.

Lacy. He heard her muffled sobs from the other room and his heart wrenched. It was time—to let go of his anger and really try to help his daughter.

Heart hammering in his chest, Walker turned and walked slowly toward her room. Outside her door, he paused and drew a deep breath. This was going to be the hardest thing he'd ever done.

Letting out his pent-up breath, he knocked. "Muffin, can I come in?" His heart turned over as she responded, her voice watery and strained from tears.

As he stepped into the room, she sat up and swiped at her eyes. He crossed and sat on the edge of the bed. "We need to talk."

She sniffed loudly. "About Alex?"

"Yes." He handed her a tissue. "But more, we need to talk about your mother."

Lacy averted her gaze and began shredding her tissue. "What do you mean?"

Walker looked down at his own hands, then back up at her. "I mean, we never really talked about how you . . . felt when your mom left." Beside him she stiffened and he hurried to add, "That was my fault, honey. I was so angry and hurt, I couldn't talk about it. That wasn't fair to you."

"It's okay, Dad." Lacy covered his hand with hers. "I love you."

He squeezed it. "I know that, Muffin. And I hope you know how much I love you. Nothing you could do or say would change that." He breathed deeply. "But how you feel about . . . your mother and loving me don't have anything to do with each other. You can love us both." He felt as if his heart might burst both with the words and the expression on her face—she looked at once fearful and hopeful and stunned. "Do you understand what I'm telling you?"

She was silent for a moment. Then she lowered her eyes and said, "I guess so. You're saying you're not mad at me for making Mom go away?"

This time tears sprang to his eyes, and he hauled Lacy into his arms and hugged her tightly. "You didn't send her away. What made you think that?"

"It was me she didn't want." Her words were muffled against his chest. "She thought I was ugly and bad. I tried to be good, but . . ."

"That's not true, sweetheart. Your mother was confused. She left us, both of us, not because she didn't love us, but because she didn't love herself." As the words passed his lips he realized they were true—and that with them his anger was gone. It was replaced by an aching sadness for what could have been and for a woman who was so desperately unhappy with herself.

"She was so pretty, everyone liked her. I don't understand."

"I know. Until this moment I didn't either." At Lacy's confused look, he tried to explain. "Some people . . ." he paused, groping for the right words, "can't see themselves as others do. Maybe they felt unloved as children, or something happened then to make them not like themselves very much. As they got older, instead of letting go of that fear and insecurity, they harbored it in their heart and—"

"And they're sad," Lacy supplied solemnly. "Like Mom."

"That's right. And that's why it's so important for us to talk about how we feel, so that we don't get confused or get the wrong idea about stuff."

"Like what I thought about why Mom left?"

"You got it."

Lacy cuddled into his side and for long moments was silent. Finally, her voice shaking, she looked up at him and said, "I love Mom so much. I wish I could make it so she would be happy."

"Me too, Muffin." He brushed the tears from her cheeks, knowing his own were wet. "Would you like to see her again?" He had to force the words past the lump in his throat.

Lacy tipped her head back and searched his face. "Do you think she wants to see me?"

"I know she does. She . . . asked me if she could."

The smile that spread across his daughter's face wrenched his heart. Alex had been right. About everything—his own inability to love and Lacy's need to express hers. Whether Lacy's narcolepsy disappeared or not, they were both healed in the way that really mattered.

Walker felt as if a crushing weight had been lifted from his shoulders. He wanted to sing, dance, shout from rooftops how he felt—happy and whole and wildly in love.

Alex would forgive him. She had to! After the way she'd badgered him about the importance of forgiveness, how could she not? He grinned. If nothing else he would shame her into it.

As if she could read his mind, Lacy looked up

at him, her eyes shining. "Does this mean I get to see Alex again?"

He stared down at her smiling face. "How did you get to be so smart?"

She giggled and jumped up. "Let's go now! I want to tell her how happy I am that she's going to be my new mom!"

"Whoa . . ." Walker dragged his daughter back down beside him. "You're getting ahead of yourself here. I won't lie, there's a chance . . . a chance, but I haven't asked her yet. We had a pretty big fight—"

"I knew it!"

"And we've never talked about marriage. She might not want me." Even as he said the words his heart plummeted to his feet. Good Lord, what would he do if she *did* say no?

"I'll go," Lacy announced, standing again and straightening her sweater. She lifted her chin importantly. "I know *I* can talk her into it."

Walker laughed. The implication that she doubted he could was clear. "That's not the way it's done, Muffin. I have to go"—at her expression, he added—"alone. She has to want me—we know she wants you."

Lacy stuck out her lower lip and looked at him as if to say "don't blow it." Walker didn't blame her, his track record wasn't so hot. "Okay," she finally said, "but hurry before someone else asks her."

Laughing, Walker did just that.

Alex was at the shop. She was sitting on the floor sifting through some stock and as he walked through the door she looked up. Their eyes met and his heart swelled with love. Just looking at her made him so happy—what if he had blown it?

His earlier confidence seemed ludicrous now and he shoved his hands into the pockets of his wool overcoat. Damn. He was scared out of his mind and had absolutely no idea of how to conquer the feeling or of what to do next. He took a deep breath and decided to start at the beginning. "Hello, Alex."

She kept her gaze fixed evenly on his. "Hello, Walker."

He shoved his hands deeper into the pockets. He'd hurt her. It was in her voice, her eyes, and the way she held herself as if the slightest breeze would snap her in two. If someone else had caused her to look that way, he would want to throttle them within an inch of their life.

He tore his gaze away from her wounded one and glanced around the shop. "Quiet today." As soon as the words were out he felt like a fool for saying them.

"Yes, but it's not unexpected." She stood and brushed off the seat of her pants, then crossed to the cash register. "Tourist season is over."

"Can you sneak away for a cup of coffee?"

She folded her arms across her chest. "I don't think so."

He winced at her tone. "Alex, we need to talk."

"Oh?"

She arched her eyebrows in a way that would have made his blue-blooded grandmother proud. It didn't do much for his own peace of mind, however, "Let me rephrase that. I need to talk. To you. Alex, I want to apologize—"

"That's not necessary." Her tone was crisp, with an edge of anger and another of indifference.

In that moment he could have believed she cared nothing for him but for her mouth. It looked soft, even bruised, and trembled slightly; it gave her face the vulnerability of a child pretending to be an adult. His heart thudded against the wall of his chest. She loved him still.

"I want, I need, to explain to you why I acted the way I did." He lowered his voice. "I want to beg your forgiveness."

She lifted her chin. "Why?"

He held her gaze. "Because I'm in love with you."

"Oh, my Lord." Alex turned her back to him, her heart beating so hard against the wall of her chest it felt as if it might burst through. She lifted a hand to the spot. She'd thought she had herself and her emotions under control. She'd thought she would be able to weather anything he could say to her. Anything but that. She squeezed her eyes shut. Could it be true? Could he really be in love with her?

"You were right, Alex. About everything—my anger, my part in Lacy's unhappiness. She thought in order to love me she couldn't love her mother. Or admit to it anyway." He paused, staring at Alex's stiff back. He wished she would look at him. When she didn't, he continued. "We talked and . . . I learned that all this time she thought she was to blame for her mother leaving."

Still Alex hadn't turned, but it seemed to him that her back wasn't as stiff, her shoulders as straight. A few of his own muscles relaxed. "Victoria Lancaster Stevenson-Ridgeman," he said softly, then repeated it, "Victoria Lancaster Stevenson-Ridgeman. I'll say her name as many times as you like, Alex. A hundred, a thousand, five thousand . . ."

Alex laughed a little, feeling lightheaded and as giddy as a schoolgirl. She was afraid to hope, but it ballooned inside her anyway. She sneaked a peek over her shoulder at him and the balloon swelled even more. He looked nervous and hopeful and uncertain. The indomitable Dr. Ridgeman was afraid. She smiled. "Can I get back to you on that?"

He returned her smile. "I made arrangements for them to get together."

"Oh, Walker . . ." She swung around then. If he could do that, his anger was gone. He was whole and free. Free to love her. Her eyes were wet. "I'm so happy for you."

"I'm happy for me too. And I want to be happy for us." He looked down at the floor for a moment, then back up at her. "But there are some things I need to say first, about the other night—"

"You don't have to, Walker. Not if you don't want to."

"Yes, I do. Your words struck a nerve. Seeing my baby that way always tears at me, I feel angry and guilty and terrified. But when the spell's over and she's asleep, I can reassure myself by blaming Victoria and telling myself I'm a good father. That night was no different. But then I found you and you hit me with 'I'm her problem' and I lost it. Maybe I did because deep down I knew it was true, maybe I wasn't even that astute and was just denying. That doesn't matter anymore. What matters is, I was unfair to you and hurt you. I'm sorry."

Alex wanted to leave well enough alone. She wanted him to enfold her in his arms, then make slow, delicious love to her. But she had to know he accepted who she was, everything she was.

She lifted her chin and steeled herself against the chance that he would say the wrong thing and she would know the truth—it would never work between them. "What about my being an empath, Walker?"

He was silent for several seconds, then looked her straight in the eye. "I'm not going to lie, as a man of science, it's hard to deal with. But you know what? It doesn't matter. I fell in love with you, Alex. Everything about you, from your crystals to your crazy hound dog. Nothing's going to change that." He held out his arms. "Are you going to make me stand here and talk forever or are you going to kiss me?"

Alex laughed and flew into his arms. "I should make you keep talking, you brute. I went through hell."

Walker pulled her against him, feeling safe for the first time in a week. "I did too. I was such an idiot not to see that I loved you."

She looped her arms around his neck. "I'll remind you of that when—"

He caught her mouth with his in a long, deep, and deliberate kiss. When it was over he smiled against her lips. "I love you, Alex."

"And I love you, Walker," she whispered, dizzy from his kiss. "I can't believe you're staying. We're going to be so happy."

"We are," he murmured, rubbing his nose against hers. "But I'm not staying. We're all going to Boston."

"Boston?"

He smiled at her surprise. "Alex, that's where my family is, my job, my home."

She drew a fraction away from him, searching his face with her eyes. "But my home's here."

"Your temporary home," he corrected, pulling her back against the wall of his chest, tangling his fingers in her hair. "You said so yourself."

Oh, Lord. Alex squeezed her eyes shut. She'd always thought in terms of him staying, never of her going with him. Now, doing so made her lightheaded. Panicky.

"Why can't you stay?" She tipped her head back so she could meet his eyes, the panic curling through her. "Think of it, a healthy, natural environment for Lacy to grow up in. A slower pace, less crime. She's flourished here, you've seen it."

He drew his eyebrows together, wondering at the edge in her voice. "Lacy's flourished with *you*, Alex. You know that. She loves you." When she didn't reply, he went on. "There's nothing for me here. I'm a surgeon, Alex, not a country doctor. I can't just hang up a shingle that says 'the doctor is in' on one side and 'gone fishing' on the other."

She flattened her hands against his chest. "I know that. But Little Rock's a good-sized town. And not a far drive. I'm sure any of the hospitals would—"

"Alex"—he caught her hands with his—"Boston General's one of the finest hospitals in the country. I won't find that in Little Rock. Lacy's grandmother and grandfather are in Boston, her cousins and aunts and uncles. I have a home, it's been in our family for generations." He brought her hands to his lips. "Come with me, Alex. Marry me. You'll love it. I know you will. It'll be the best thing for us."

Go with him to Boston? Be a society wife? Like her mother had been? Her stomach muscles tightened as she thought of her childhood and of trying to mold herself into something she was not. She'd been a dismal failure at it and miserable in the process.

Suddenly she felt the way she had the day of her bridal shower. Suffocated, as if she'd been stuffed into an ill-fitting suit. And the feeling hadn't gone away until she'd faced the truth about herself and what she needed.

She slipped her hands out of his and stepped outside of the circle of his arms. She couldn't say what she had to if he was touching her. She sucked in a steadying breath. "I can't, Walker. I'm sorry."

Walker took an involuntary step backward, as if she'd punched him. He must have misheard her, he thought, staring at her blankly. But he hadn't, he saw it in her eyes. "Don't you love me?"

"Lord, yes. So much it hurts."

"Then what's the problem?" He caught her hands again and squeezed. "You could work . . . or you could do nothing. I have a household staff so you wouldn't be saddled with those kinds of responsibilities, there are art galleries and museums, there's the theater and great shopping. I know you'd love it. I know you would. You're just scared."

"You're doing the same thing my parents did to me. Telling me *you* know what's right for me, telling me how *I* feel." She swung away from him, fighting to control her tears. "I can't even manage my hair let alone a household staff. Can you imagine me giving a tea? Or even attending one? Dear Lord, your mother would take one look at me and have a coronary." The tears threatened to spill over, and she blinked furiously. "I'd hurt your career instead of help it."

"It doesn't matter."

She shook her head, the tears winning and slipping down her cheeks. "It does. It would. We'd both end up unhappy."

"I don't expect you to be anything but who you are. I fell in love with *you*, Alex. Not a socialite, a Boston blueblood, or even a southern belle. You, Alex."

"You fell in love with me *here*. Take me out of context and—"

"You're wrong."

"Am I? You say that now. But I saw my mother, what she had to do, to be. You're an important man, from an important family. Certain things are expected from the wife of a man in your position. Things like knowing how to entertain—and I don't mean chips and dip and whatever wine was on sale. Things like being able to mix with the right people while saying the right things and wearing the right clothes. What happens the first time you need me to organize a benefit for the hospital? Or entertain the board? Do you think they'll be so understanding of your kooky wife?"

She imagined the expressions of his associates if they saw her in hiking boots and covered with sulphur and red clay, and she laughed, the sound high and tight. "Sure, this is the nineties, and women are doing and being a lot of different things. But Atlanta's a lot like Boston in that tradition is important. They would accept me if I was a doctor myself or a lawyer. But an empath, healer, and crystal merchant?"

She wiped at the moisture on her cheeks. "I

could change or keep my mouth shut about my beliefs. I could learn how to dress for success and throw a five-star party—and a big part of me is screaming to do just that—but that wouldn't be me, and it wouldn't be honest. I'd be doing what I did as a child, and I'd be miserable."

"You're not being fair," Walker said slowly, a catch in his voice. "It's either love you here or not at all?"

"Are you being fair?" she shot back. "Aren't you saying exactly the same thing?"

"What about Lacy? She loves you, you know. She thinks I'm coming back to the cottage to tell her about her new mom. She'll be devastated."

Alex blanched. For a moment she thought it might even be worth it—her identity in exchange for Walker and Lacy. If she didn't know from experience it wouldn't work, she'd give it a shot. But if she did, in the end, she would only hurt Lacy more. "Don't," she murmured, her voice shaking. "I love her so much . . . I can't bear to think of making her unhappy."

"Then don't. Come with us."

"Using the way I feel about your daughter is low, Walker."

"And I'd do it again." He grabbed her upper arms, forcing her to look at him. "I love you, you love me; it should be simple."

She shook her head. "Believe me, Walker, I'm saving us all a lot of future heartache."

He dropped his hands. "I can't believe this is good-bye."

Alex drew in a shaking breath. "It doesn't have to be. You can stay. Or, I'll be here, Walker. I love you . . . you can come—"

"And we can be part-time, whenever I can break

away, lovers? No thanks. I've learned something, Alex. I need more than that, Lacy needs more than that. She needs a mother, she needs a woman in her life who's there all the time to care for and love her. We both want you to be that woman, but if you won't . . ."

His meaning was clear and Alex curled her fingers into her palms. Walker loving another woman, Lacy calling that woman Mom. She felt as if she might die from the pain the images brought.

She looked up at him. Maybe she was making a mistake, maybe she could make it work. Once again she thought of the past, of how unhappy she'd been, and it seemed as if there wasn't enough air in the room. In the end she was saving them all a lot of heartache. "Then, I guess this is good-bye."

Without another word, Walker turned and walked out of the shop.

Eleven

Today was the day. Alexis Stanton Clare drew in a deep breath and squared her shoulders. She *could* do it. Turning to the side, she clipped the leash onto Heinz's collar, opened the car door and slipped out with the dog right behind her.

She tightened her fingers on the leash as she stared up at the Back Bay brownstone, the one that had been in Walker's family for generations. Even as she told herself to walk to the door, she stood rooted to the spot, scared silly.

What if he didn't want her anymore? What if he'd found the other woman he'd threatened he would the last time they'd seen each other?

Alex pushed the thoughts away. It had taken her a month and a half of pure misery to get this far. If she fixated on all the "what ifs" she would never cross the twelve feet of pavement in front of her.

Alex stared at the pavement, thinking of those forty-five days. The panicky sensation, the feeling of not being able to breathe that had begun the day Walker proposed, had not only lingered, it'd grown worse. Instead of feeling free and whole she had felt lost and somehow fractured.

Hungry for something she couldn't put her finger on, she'd called her mother. Alex lifted her lips in wry amusement. Funny how the sound of her mother's cultured voice had made her realize things she hadn't been able to on her own. Things like she'd been so afraid of losing herself that she'd completely closed herself off from the possibility of real happiness. The kind she could have with Walker and Lacy.

The kind her mother wanted for her. Alex smiled. For the first time ever, she'd heard the message underlying her mother's criticisms— above all, she wanted her daughter to be happy.

Breathing deeply, Alex tipped her face up to the sky. The air was different in Boston. Not as clean, but crisp and somehow busier. People hurried by her and although they glanced her way, they didn't look at her as if she was wrong or didn't fit in.

It would be fine here, Alex thought confidently, *she* would be fine.

As she took a step forward, the front door of the brownstone swung open and Walker and Lacy stepped out. Her confidence evaporated, and her stomach crashed to her toes.

Even as she fought the urge to run, longing, so poignant it left her aching, curled through her. Anyone passing would know Walker and Lacy were father and daughter; they would see how happy there were, how much they adored each other. She swallowed. They looked as if the last thing they needed in their lives was a crazy red-head and her equally goofy dog.

She wasn't ready for this, she thought, taking a step backward. She needed a few more seconds, even days. She needed to prepare . . .

Lacy saw her first.

"Alex!"

Worries about "what ifs" and not being prepared flew out of her mind as the child barreled down the stairs, her arms out. "Lacy!" Alex dropped her tote bag and the leash and held her own arms out. She caught the girl to her, hugging her tightly, the knot of tears in her chest so big she didn't think she could hold them back.

"I knew you'd come," Lacy said, clutching her. "I knew it!"

"I missed you so much." Alex buried her face in Lacy's hair, breathing in the sweet, little-girl scent she remembered so well. What would she do if Walker no longer wanted her? Saying a silent prayer, she lifted her eyes once again to the brownstone.

Walker was too stunned to move. He'd thought he'd never see her again. She was wearing an old down-filled coat, jeans that had probably seen the late seventies and her terrible hiking boots. She looked as if she'd pulled an all-nighter. He'd never seen a woman look better.

He squeezed his eyes shut for one moment, then reopened them. If this was anything but what he hoped it was, he would wring her beautiful neck. "Hello, Alex."

Heart thundering in her chest and palms sweating, she tried a smile. She was shaking so badly, she could barely get her lips to respond. "Hello, Walker."

Lacy whirled around to her father. "Dad, it's Alex! Didn't I tell you she'd come? And she brought Heinz!" The dog whined at his name, and Lacy threw herself at him. He immediately covered her face with slobbery kisses. "I missed you, Heinz! You're going to love it here. I promise!"

The words were too familiar and Walker dragged his gaze from Alex to his daughter and back. "Will he, Alex? Will he be happy here?"

Alex realized then that even her insides were shaking. She straightened her shoulders and lifted her chin. It was either that or crumble. "If you'll let him stay."

Walker stared at her, she stared back. One second stretched into two, stretched into a dozen. He didn't smile, but neither did she. In that time, she wasn't sure she even breathed.

Walker spoke first. "Lacy, take Heinz for a walk."

"Can I take him over to Gram's?"

Walker didn't take his eyes from Alex. "That's a great idea, Muffin. In fact, tell her you have to stay for supper."

"But I don't wa . . ." Her words trailed off as she looked at her father, then at Alex. She stood and brushed off her coat, trying to act adult and nonchalant. "Oh, sure. Gram'll like that. She doesn't have any pets of her own."

As Lacy and Heinz started off, Walker started down the steps. Still Alex didn't move. She told herself to, but couldn't seem to follow her own orders. With every step closer he came to her, her heart beat faster. When he finally stopped in front of her, she thought it might burst through her chest.

His eyes were as deep and velvety a brown as before, his hair just as thick and curly as it had been. But he looked changed anyway—a little thinner, a little older and wiser, a bit drawn. She lifted a hand to his cheek. He'd recently shaved and it was smooth under her palm. She sucked in a sharp breath; she couldn't have imagined such a simple caress could be so fulfilling. She was home.

Alex searched his expression for a clue to how he felt. He wasn't giving anything away. "Lacy probably thinks we're going to be kissing and stuff," she whispered, despising the quaver in her voice.

He turned his face into her palm and pressed his lips there, then covered her hand with his. "She's probably right."

Alex let out a long breath, sweet relief washing over her. It was going to be all right. She smiled. "I'll take that as a good sign."

He smiled at her but released her hand. "Do you have a suitcase?"

"Only one," she said. "I thought I would go back for everything else . . . if you still"—she cleared her throat—"if I was staying."

Wordlessly, Walker hauled it out of the back end of the jeep, then motioned to the brownstone. Hugging her tote bag to her chest, she followed him across the pavement and up the front steps.

Walker dropped the suitcase just inside the door. Alex stepped cautiously across the threshold and looked around her. No place could be more different from her cabin. His home was beautiful, a showplace. There was important art, fine bric-a-brac and what looked to be authentic and costly antiques everywhere. The ceilings were high, the wood floors shiny and unmarred. She shuddered as she thought of Heinz skidding across them.

"Come on, I'll show you to your room."

Alex arched her brows at both his formality and at the fact she would have her own room, one that was different from his. Something was wrong, she thought, panicked. He didn't love her anymore and was only waiting for the right moment to tell her he'd changed his—

"Alex?"

She looked up in dismay. He was halfway up the staircase already. Once again trying to smile, she hurried after him.

The second level was as elegantly furnished and immaculately maintained as the first. She'd known it would be but had hoped for just a bit of chaos anyway. Her hands trembled, and she gripped the handle of her tote so tightly her knuckles turned white.

Walker entered a bedroom with an antique four-poster bed and a small chintz-covered sofa. The armoire in the corner appeared to be the same style as the bed and was huge. It was a warm, welcoming kind of room. She felt lost.

Walker came up behind her, stopping so close she could feel his breath stir against her hair, but didn't touch her.

"You're quiet," he said softly.

She squeezed her eyes shut. "I'm scared."

"Of me?"

She turned, adrenaline racing through her. "Of losing you."

He stared at her a moment, then cupped her face in his palms. "No chance."

"Then why were you so quiet?" Her voice shook

slightly. "I thought you were figuring out ways to tell me to take a hike."

Walker laughed. "I was in shock—I still am." He feathered his lips across her eyelids, her cheeks, down the curve of her neck. He groaned and set her away from him. "That's not completely true, Alex. I was scared, too, out of my mind scared. I thought you'd take one look at this place and run or that I'd say the wrong thing and . . ." He shook his head. "The last weeks have been hell. I can't go through it again. If this isn't forever, go now and don't come back."

Tears sprang to her eyes. At his words, but more at the truth behind them—she had hurt him deeply. "I'm not going anywhere."

"Oh, Alex." He hauled her against his chest and caught her mouth. It was as soft and sweet as he remembered, she tasted the same—like spring-time and laughter. But there was a possessiveness in the way she held him now, a freedom in the way she responded. Both reassured in a way words never would. He pushed her coat off her shoulders.

Alex pressed herself against him, burying her fingers in his thick, dark hair. How had she thought she would lose herself in Walker? He was half of what she was, without him she would never be whole. She'd been such a fool!

She pulled free of his arms and turned to face him. "I want to make love to you, Walker. I want to feel you inside me so I'll know, really know, that we're together again. But I need to talk first." She smiled softly. "Once I'm in your arms I won't be able to think, let alone describe to you what happened to me in the last month and a half."

"You don't have to tell me a thing, not if you

don't want to. You say you're going to stay, that's enough for me."

He'd changed, she realized, more than she could have imagined. He believed in her wholly, without suspicions or guarantees. "Thank you, Walker." She pressed her lips to his, then pulled out of his arms. "I need to tell you because I hurt you and Lacy. I want to share this with you because I want to share everything with you, because I love you."

Alex laced her fingers together. "I was attracted to you from the first time I saw you. I told myself I fought the attraction for a lot of reasons other than the real one . . . I was afraid."

Walker tenderly touched her cheek. "Of me? I'm a pussycat."

. She smiled a little at that, then lowered her eyes. "No, not of you." She looked at him again. "I wasn't like the rest of my family, I never fit in. They had expectations for me that I tried to meet but couldn't. It was an awful way to feel—like I was always disappointing them, like the prover-bial square peg. So I left 'to find myself.' " She laughed self-consciously. "Lord, that sounds so clichéd."

She swung away from him. "I thought Hot Springs was part of who I am, I thought to be me I couldn't compromise even one thought. In truth, I was still running. Hot Springs was com-fortable. A good hiding place."

Alex faced him again. "You told me once that *I* had to face my fears. You were right. I almost lost you because I was afraid I wouldn't fit in here, in your world. I was terrified *I* would contort myself to fit because I loved you and because I would want desperately to belong."

"And now?" he asked quietly.

"Now I know love is belonging." She laughed. "And compromising is giving and to be me . . . I just be me."

"Turns out we both needed healing," Walker murmured, moving her into his arms and lowering her gently to the mattress.

She trailed her fingers across his lips. "Without you I might never have realized it."

He caught the finger in a gentle nip. "We healed each other."

Tears welled in her eyes, then spilled over. The Walker Ridgeman she'd first met would never have said that. "I love you."

He caught one of her tears with his mouth. "I love you too."

They removed each other's clothes, murmuring their love, their appreciation, for each other as they did. Their lovemaking was tender, quiet, not at all what Alex had imagined it would be like when they first got back together, but infinitely more moving. She had never felt so loved, so cherished. She knew Walker felt the same: It was in his eyes as he looked at her, his hands as he caressed her, in the way he called to her as he reached the peak and crested it.

Enfolded in each other's embrace and totally content, the minutes ticked by until the light slanting through the window had changed direction then dimmed. Walker stirred. "Alex?"

"Hmm?"

He brushed his lips across the top of her head. "I thought you were sleeping."

She stretched, then cuddled closer into his side. "I thought you were."

"I was listening to you breathe."

She tipped her head back and smiled at him. "I was listening to you."

"I like that." He placed a kiss on the tip of her nose. "I want to thank you again for what you did for Lacy. She's doing so well. She only has an occasional sleep attack and cataplexic spell, but more miraculous than that is the way she feels about herself and life. She's happier, more carefree, and has lots of friends her own age now."

"I'm glad." Alex leaned on her elbow and looked at him, drawing her eyebrows together. "She saw her mother?"

"A couple of times. I don't know what the ending to that story's going to be, Victoria is as scattered as ever. I hope she gets some counseling; she deserves some happiness."

"Oh, Walker."

He grinned and rolled her over, pinning her under him. "You know, speaking of Lacy, I suspect my mother had a heart attack when she saw Heinz. I also suspect dinner will be hurried and that we'll have visitors . . . soon."

"What!" Alex pushed at his chest. "Wait until she sees me!"

"She'll adore you."

"She'll hate me!" When brute force didn't work, Alex tried to shimmy out of his arms. "I need to clean up. First impressions are so important! Walker"—she glared at him—"let me up."

He ran his hand along the smooth curve of her hip, then lower. "We have time."

A tingle raced up her spine. She steeled herself against it and squirmed. When he moved his other hand, she sighed and gave up, sagging against him. "How do you know?"

"They'll call first. After all, it's the polite, civilized thing to do."

Alex thought about that for a minute, then laughed and moved her own hands. "Predictability can be a wonderful thing."

At the same moment he caught her mouth, the phone rang. Walker smiled wickedly against her lips. "Let it ring."

Alex didn't argue.

THE EDITOR'S CORNER

In publishing a series such as LOVESWEPT we couldn't function without timetables, schedules, deadlines. It seems we're always working toward one, only to reach it then strive for another. I mention the topic because many of you write and ask us questions about the way we work and about how and when certain books are published. Just consider this Editor's Corner as an example. I'm writing this in early April, previewing our October books, which will run in our September books, which will be on sale in August. The books you're reading about were scheduled for publication at least nine months earlier and were probably written more than a year before they reach your hands! Six books a month means seventy-two a year, and we're into our seventh year of publication. That's a lot of books and a lot of information to try to keep up with. Amazingly, we do keep up—and so do our authors. We enjoy providing you with the answer to a question about a particular book or author or character. Your letters mean a lot to us.

In our ongoing effort to extend the person-to-person philosophy of LOVESWEPT, we are setting up a 900 number through which you can learn what's new—and what's old—with your favorite authors! Next month's Editor's Corner will have the full details for you.

Kay Hooper's most successful series for us to date has been her *Once Upon a Time . . .* novels. These modern-day fairy tales have struck a chord with you, the readers, and your enjoyment of the books has delighted and inspired Kay. Her next in this series is LOVESWEPT #426, **THE LADY AND THE LION,** and it's one of Kay's sizzlers. Keith Donovan and Erin Prentice first speak to each other from their adjacent hotel balconies, sharing secrets and desperate murmurings in the dark. Kay creates a moody, evocative, emotionally charged atmosphere in which these two kindred spirits fall in love before they ever meet. But when they finally do set eyes on each other, they know without having to speak that they've found their destinies. This wonderful story will bring out the true romantic in all of you!

We take you from fairy tales to fairyland this month! Our next LOVESWEPT, #427, **SATIN SHEETS AND STRAWBERRIES** by Marcia Evanick, features a golden-haired nymph of a heroine named Kelli SantaFe. Hero Logan Sinclair does a double take when he arrives at what looks like Snow White's cottage in search of his aunt and uncle—and finds a bewitching woman dressed as a fairy. Kelli runs her business from her home and at first resents Logan's interference and the tug-of-war he wages for his relatives, whom she'd taken in and treated like the family

(continued)

she'd always wanted. Logan is infuriated by her stubbornness, yet intrigued by the woman who makes him feel as though his feet barely touch the ground. Kelli falls hard for Logan, who can laugh at himself and rescue damsels in distress, but who has the power to shatter her happiness. You'll find you're enchanted by the time Kelli and Logan discover how to weave their dreams together!

All of us feel proud and excited whenever we publish a new author in the line. The lady whose work we're introducing you to next month is a talented, hardworking mother of five who strongly believes in the importance of sprinkling each day with a little romance. We think Olivia Rupprecht does just that with **BAD BOY OF NEW ORLEANS**, LOVESWEPT #428. I don't know about you, but some of my all-time favorite romances involve characters who reunite after years apart. I find these stories often epitomize the meaning of true love. Well, in **BAD BOY OF NEW ORLEANS** Olivia reunites two people whose maddening hunger for each other has only deepened with time. Hero Chance Renault can still make Micah Sinclair tremble, can still make her burn for his touch and cry out for the man who had loved her first. But over time they've both changed, and a lot stands between them. Micah feels she must prove she can survive on her own, while Chance insists she belongs to him body and soul. Their journey toward happiness together is one you won't want to miss!

Joan Elliott Pickart never ceases to amaze me with the way she is able to provide us with winning romance after winning romance. She's truly a phenomenon, and we're pleased and honored to bring you her next LOVESWEPT, #429, **STORMING THE CASTLE**. While reunited lovers have their own sets of problems to overcome, when two very different people find themselves falling in love, their long-held beliefs, values, and lifestyles become an issue. In **STORMING THE CASTLE**, Dr. Maggie O'Leary finds her new hunk of a neighbor, James-Steven Payton, to be a free spirit, elusive as the wind and just as irresistible. Leave it to him to choose the unconventional over the customary way of doing things. But Maggie grew up with a father who was much the same, whose devil-may-care ways often brought heartache. James-Steven longs to see the carefree side of Maggie, and he sets out to get her to smell the flowers and to build sand castles without worrying that the tide will wash them away. Though Maggie longs to join her heart to his, she knows they must first find a common ground. Joan handles this tender story beautifully. It's a real heart-warmer!

One author who always delivers a fresh, innovative story is Mary Kay McComas. Each of her LOVESWEPTs is unique and imaginative—never the same old thing! In **FAVORS**, LOVESWEPT #430, Mary Kay has once again let her creative juices flow, and

(continued)

the result is a story unlike any other. Drawing on her strength in developing characters you come to know intimately and completely, Mary Kay serves up a romance filled with emotion and chock full of fun. Her tongue-in-cheek portrayal of several secondary characters will have you giggling, and her surprise ending will add the finishing touch to your enjoyment of the story. When agent Ian Walker is asked to protect a witness as a favor to his boss, he considers the job no more appealing than baby-sitting—until he meets Trudy Babbitt, alias Pollyanna. The woman infuriates him by refusing to believe she's in danger—and ignites feelings in him he'd thought were long dead. Trudy sees beneath Ian's crusty exterior and knows she can transform him with her love. But first they have to deal with the reality of their situation. I don't want to give away too much, so I'll just suggest you keep in mind while reading **FAVORS** that nothing is exactly as it seems. Crafty Mary Kay pulls a few aces from her sleeve!

One of your favorite authors—and ours—Billie Green returns to our lineup next month with **SWEET AND WILDE**, #431. Billie has always been able to capture that indefinable quality that makes a LOVESWEPT romance special. In her latest for us, she throws together an unlikely pair of lovers, privileged Alyson Wilde and streetwise Sid Sweet and sends them on an incredible adventure. You might wonder what a blue-blooded lady could have in common with a bail bondsman and pawnshop owner, but Billie manages to keep her characters more than a little bit interested in each other. When thirteen-year-old Lenny, who is Alyson's ward, insists that his friend Sid Sweet is a great guy and role model, Alyson decides she has to meet the tough-talking man for herself. And cynical Sid worries that Good Samaritan Alyson has taken Lenny on only as her latest "project." With Lenny's best interests at heart, they go with him in search of his past and end up discovering their own remarkable future—one filled with a real love that is better than any of their fantasies.

Be sure to pick up all six books next month. They're all keepers!

Sincerely,

Susann Brailey

Susann Brailey
Editor
LOVESWEPT
Bantam Books
666 Fifth Avenue
New York, NY 10103